A
Harlequin
Romance

A STRANGER IS MY LOVE

OTHER
Harlequin Romances
by MARGARET MALCOLM

Many of these titles are available at your local bookseller,
or through the Harlequin Reader Service.

For a free catalogue listing all available Harlequin Romances,
send your name and address to:

HARLEQUIN READER SERVICE,
M.P.O. Box 707, Niaga a Falls, N.Y. 14302
Canadian address: Stratford, Ontario, Canada N5A 6W4

or use coupon at back of books.

A STRANGER
IS MY LOVE

by

MARGARET MALCOLM

HARLEQUIN BOOKS   TORONTO
WINNIPEG

Original hard cover edition published
by Mills & Boon Limited

SBN 373-01934-3

Harlequin edition published December 1975

Printed in Canada

1934

CHAPTER ONE

EVEN with the two doors shut, Karen could still hear the harsh, angry voices speaking in the dining-room.

She had tried clattering the crockery that she was washing up, but even that had not drowned the ugly sound.

And Karen hated anger. It was one of the things that frightened her — particularly when, as now, she knew that it was because of her that they were angry.

She put away the last of the heavy, old-fashioned cutlery into its green-baize-lined drawers and slowly untied her apron. From sheer force of habit, she folded it neatly and placed it in its own little nook. Then she remembered and took it out again. What was the use of putting it there when she would never need it again? At least, not in that house.

There was nothing else for her to do but wait. Odd that, in a house where for four years she had been busy from morning to night — and sometimes into the night as well.

Poor old Miss Cotton with her old, pain-racked body and her unhappy, malicious mind! So rich. And yet so poor and lonely. She had hated her relatives. Vultures, she had called them. And now that she had met them, Karen saw that she had not been entirely wrong.

For Miss Cotton was dead. And this was the day of the funeral. So all the relatives who had been told that they were not wanted here by Miss Cotton had come because there was no longer anyone with the power to keep them away. They had come for something else as well. Never, in all her long life, had Miss Cotton let a single word drop as to her choice of heir or heirs.

And that was why Karen knew quite well why they had looked at her with such suspicion and dislike in their calculating eyes. She was only about a fifth cousin, several times removed from Miss Cotton, but for four years she had been the only one who had been in close association with the sick old woman. And who knew what influence

7

she had exerted and how much money she had persuaded Miss Cotton to leave her?

Karen alone knew the truth, which she had promised Miss Cotton faithfully she would not divulge during her lifetime. She herself was to have exactly one hundred pounds. Every other single penny was to be devoted to cancer research work. Not a single relative benefited.

"And I'd like to see them getting anything out of the cancer people," Miss Cotton had said with malicious glee. "Or saying I'm out of my mind — when it's cancer that I'm dying of."

And now they knew. That was why their voices were so loud and so angry. Even Mr. Pilbright, the little solicitor who looked so dry that he must rattle if you shook him, had had to raise his voice almost to a shout to make himself heard.

And then a door slammed. A moment later the kitchen door opened as if a typhoon had hit it. And Mr. Pilbright came in.

Karen's hands, that had been lying loosely in her lap, linked and gripped. She looked up at Mr. Pilbright's flushed, angry face with anxious eyes.

"Were they very cross?" she asked falteringly.

Mr. Pilbright laughed drily.

"My dear girl, you have a positive genius for understatement," he commented. "Cross? They were absolutely livid!"

"Miss Cotton said that there was nothing they could do about it," Karen said a little breathlessly.

"To upset the will, you mean?" he said. "Quite right. It is a perfectly sound, watertight will. Your hundred is absolutely safe."

Karen flushed.

"I wasn't thinking of that," she said reproachfully.

"Well, you should be," he retorted bluntly. "It's all that there is between you and the gutter."

"I know." There was a quake of fear in her voice that she could not control and, for a moment, the elderly solicitor and the young girl stared at one another.

She saw a prim, withered little man in immaculate but old-fashioned clothes whose cut-and-dried appearance was oddly at variance with his present agitation.

What he saw was a young girl who could not have left her teens very far behind her, with grey, frightened eyes set in the pale, oval face of a Madonna. Her hair was dark, almost black; a smooth frame that made her face still paler.

"You'll have to get another job." He spoke sharply because he was annoyed with the feeling of responsibility that this thin, immature girl awakened in him. "Got anything in mind?"

"I wondered if any of them in there wanted help — with children or elderly people," she said timidly.

"They did," he told her grimly. "But I soon scotched that!"

"Oh, but why?" Her smooth forehead furrowed anxiously. "I must work. And one job is much like another."

"Not of a necessity," he said slowly. "In any case, I wouldn't let my worst enemy work for Emma Crask. Let alone an unprotected child like you."

She flashed him a grateful glance that had the effect of lighting up her whole face. For the first time he saw the possibilities of beauty in it. And it made him feel more confident about a plan that he had all but discarded as impossible.

"Is Mrs. Crask the fat one or the thin one?" she asked without much interest.

"The one with the fishy eyes," he said as abstractedly. "A nagger and a slave-driver, if ever there was one. And the children are little devils. Except the eldest son. He is a big devil. He would probably try to flirt with you. No; you can't go there."

There was a little pause.

"But I *must* have a job," she insisted. "And there is so little that I am capable of doing. So it doesn't do to start picking and choosing."

"Yes, it does," he contradicted flatly. "If you have a commodity to sell that other people want."

"But have I?" she said wistfully. "I can only do the things that other people can do themselves — cook and nurse, or perhaps I could help with children. At school I was always at the bottom of the form."

"It isn't every woman that can cook and nurse," he

insisted. "At least, not properly. But, in any case, there are other things — for a woman. Marriage, for example."

From behind thick glasses, his small dark eyes watched her closely. And, somehow or other, it did not greatly surprise him that she shrank back.

"Oh, *no!*" she breathed, her dark eyes dilating.

"Good heavens, why not?" he demanded. "I thought all girls were determined to get married."

"Are they?" she said indifferently. "I don't know. I haven't had much to do with other girls since I left school."

"And didn't they ever talk about boy friends?" he asked curiously.

"I think they did," she said simply. "But not to me."

He glanced thoughtfully at the still-childish face and the innocent eyes and nodded.

"No; I suppose not. All the same, I wouldn't put it beyond the bounds of possibility that you might marry — one of these days," he added hastily as he saw her look of startled apprehension.

"If," she began slowly, smoothing her shabby cotton dress with work-roughened hands, "if there was someone that I could always trust to be — to be kind. But how would one know? You have to be with people a lot before you are quite sure that you really know what they are like, don't you?"

"What do you mean by being kind?" he fenced, avoiding answering one question by asking another.

She frowned in an effort of concentration.

"I couldn't *bear* to marry anyone who was rude to me in public," she said at last. "And married people so often are. I've heard them. It makes me tighten up inside."

"It does me, too," Mr. Pilbright admitted, looking at her with growing interest. "I've often noticed it. There is no class of people more inclined to be unpleasantly outspoken than husbands and wives. Almost as if the fact of the relationship forces them to be. One of the reasons why I've never risked entering the holy state! Go on!"

"Oh — it is so difficult to put it into words," she protested. "If it were truly 'love, honour and cherish,' I think it might be all right. But suppose it wasn't! You couldn't just give notice. It's until death us do part, you know."

He turned away sharply and contemplated the over-coloured tradesman's calendar on the wall with disproportionate interest.

"Yes, just so," he said reflectively. "Well — anyhow; I've got a job in view for you. It may do for you; it may not. We'll see. In the meantime, go and pack. I'm not leaving you to the tender mercies of these wolves and vultures for five minutes. They'd skin you of that hundred pounds in half the time! Oh, it's quite all right. My sister lives with me. Keeps house for me, in fact. So it's quite proper. Now hurry, if you please!"

He spoke a little crossly because he had never in this wide world meant to make such a suggestion, but there honestly seemed nothing else to do, and he hoped to goodness that Eleanor would understand. You never quite knew where you were with women, even the best of them.

Karen went slowly upstairs. Past the door of what had been Miss Cotton's room. Past the door of the room that had been hers until a few days ago so that she could hear Miss Cotton if she called in the night. But with all the relations staying in the house for the funeral, she had bundled all her odds and ends of belongings out of the second-best room into the tiny attic on the top floor. She went slowly up to it for the last time; pausing halfway up because she was a little bit breathless. Poor Miss Cotton had been very demanding these last few weeks and she was tired with all the running about that there had been. It was rather frightening. To be so tired when you are only twenty-two and have to earn your own living.

She would not need to keep Mr. Pilbright waiting long, because, realising that she could not continue living in this ugly, inconvenient old house, she had already packed practically everything. She brushed her hair smooth with a shabby old brush on which half the letter 'R' clung in a thin twist of battered silver. It stood for Rosamund and it had been her mother's. Rosamund! That was a lovely name, she thought, as she had so often thought before. The sort of name that a girl whom everybody loved would have. Actually, she knew practically nothing about either of her parents. Her father had died before she was born and her mother soon after she had given birth to the little

11

daughter who had been labelled with the outlandish name of Karenhappuch because it was a good Biblical name, and no one bothered to think how she might feel about it when she grew up.

"Are you coming?" demanded Mr. Pilbright from the foot of the stairs and, with a guilty start, Karen called, "Coming!" and bundled the last of her possessions into the shabby case. Then she hurried downstairs, and Mr. Pilbright, watching her, felt his heart sink. She'd never do! Damn it, what he was looking for was a clever, sophisticated girl who knew how to cope with difficulties, not a narrow-chested child who looked like an awkward fledgling in that skimpy black outfit: a little black crow.

Perhaps she read something of the doubts in his mind, for she suddenly stopped and faltered:

"Perhaps — I'd better not come. I shall be a nuisance——"

He heard the wistful note in her voice and saw the trembling lip. And it was too much for him.

"Nonsense!" he said crossly because he objected to being so moved. "Come along and don't waste any more of my time!"

Obediently she followed him, but in the gaunt-looking hall with its crudely tessellated floor and hideous stained glass windows he paused.

"Look here," he said, sniffing irresolutely. "No need to go out of the front door, is there? I mean, they are bound to see us. Might make a fuss. What about the back door?"

She looked at him in amazement. It couldn't — simply couldn't be that Mr. Pilbright was afraid of the relations just as she was? But he was! Suddenly her lips curved into a delicious, conspiratorial smile. She put out her hand and took his dry one in it. Then, together, they tiptoed out through the kitchen and so to the back door and the little garden path that led to a door in the garden wall.

Karen closed it carefully behind them and turned to her confederate. He had removed his hard felt hat and was mopping his forehead.

"Phew!" he whistled. "The worst five minutes I've ever had! Suppose they'd caught us!"

Then he saw the twinkle in Karen's eyes and, once he

had got over the surprise of seeing it there, began to laugh. But he stopped again quickly because Karen, too, had begun to laugh. And never in his life had he heard such a lovely sound. It made him think of wind-bells and crystal lustres and little bubbling streams — he could have listened indefinitely. But Karen became serious again.

"We had better go," she suggested. "There is a train in a quarter of an hour. We could just catch it."

Eleanor Pilbright may have been both surprised and annoyed at having an unexpected guest on her hands but, if so, she did not admit it. In fact, she announced that Karen's room was waiting for her in a voice not wholly devoid of triumph.

"Anyone would think you knew I was bringing her," Mr. Pilbright said irritably.

"Of course I did, Aubrey!" his sister told him. "I knew your heart is too soft not to look after the poor child!"

"It's nothing of the sort!" he said indignantly. "I'm a hard, professional man. Nothing more and nothing less."

Miss Pilbright sniffed unbelievingly and turned to Karen.

"You look as if you ought to go to bed for a week," she commented. "But I expect you're young enough for a night's rest to put you straight! Come with me and see your room!"

Karen followed her in silence, too tired to take much notice of her surroundings and yet vaguely conscious of that indefinable atmosphere of a real home.

There was a gas fire burning in her room and the bed was invitingly turned down.

"Now," Miss Pilbright said firmly, "I am going to tuck you in bed and bring you up some beef-tea. Yes, I know it is early, but you shall come down later if you feel like it. And, in the meantime, if you are sensible, you will admit that it is just what you would like to do!"

"It is," Karen admitted, trying to swallow the little lump that would come into her throat because she was not used to people being kind and considerate to her.

"Very well then!" Miss Pilbright said briskly. "I'll go down and get the beef-tea, and mind you're in bed when I come back."

Obediently, Karen slipped into her cotton nightdress and got into bed. Her toes touched a hot-water bottle and she snuggled down with a little sigh of sheer bliss. The future might hold all sorts of problems, but for the moment she was too tired and too comfortable to think about them.

When Miss Pilbright came back, she was already fast asleep.

For a moment the thin, angular woman stood watching her. Then she went slowly downstairs and rejoined her brother.

"Well?" he demanded.

She shook her head.

"I don't know, Aubrey. I don't know," she said slowly.

"There is a strong likeness," he insisted.

"Yes," she admitted. "From that point of view — perhaps. No!" she said suddenly, her tone positive. "There is nothing more than skin-deep likeness. For the rest, she's exquisitely sensitive — too much so for her own comfort!"

"Ah!" He sounded pleased. "You saw that, too. Well, mightn't that be a good thing?"

She shook her head.

"How do I know?" she said distractedly. "How do you? Well, at least promise me one thing, Aubrey!"

"That I won't try to over-influence her?" he asked and she nodded. "No; I won't do that. I promise you!"

Karen woke up the next morning to find the sun pouring into her room. She lay quite still for a minute as the recollection of all that had happened since the same time yesterday poured into her mind with the stunning force of a river in spate.

It was incredible! Then she had been completely alone. Nobody had cared tuppence about her. Now, though she was in a strange house, she was surrounded by the atmosphere of affection and consideration. She looked about the room. It was rather old-fashioned, but Karen, knowing very little about modern development in furnishing, saw nothing to criticise in that. The curtains were blue-and-white chintz, and so was the quilt that lay neatly folded over the back of a chair. The crockery on the washstand carried the blue-and-white colour scheme one step further and there was a blue-and-white carpet on the floor: Indian, although Karen did not know that. There were two white vases holding blue flowers on the mantelpiece and a little china clock with forget-me-nots painted on it. For a moment Karen only regarded this with general interest. Then, suddenly, she realised that the hands pointed to ten o'clock!

With a little exclamation of horror, she jumped out of bed. But she had got no further than scrambling into her shabby old kimono when there was a gentle knock at the door and Miss Pilbright came in bearing a tray.

"Ah, so you're awake," she said pleasantly. "I didn't disturb you with an early morning cup of tea because I thought it would do you more good to sleep on. Now, pop back into bed and eat this all up!"

Karen scrambled back into bed because she was so used to doing what she was told that it did not occur to her to do anything else, but her eyes were troubled.

"I *am* so sorry I am putting you to all this trouble," she said a little anxiously. "Truly, I've only just woken up."

"My dear little girl, you could not have pleased me better than by resting," Miss Pilbright assured her as she settled the tray on Karen's knees. "Now I'll light the fire. These early October mornings are bright, but there is not very much warmth in the sun."

"Oh, please," Karen said quickly. "Don't worry about it. I'm not used to a fire in my bedroom."

"No; I suppose not," Miss Pilbright agreed, serenely going about her self-appointed task. "That seems to me all the more reason why you should have one now! Besides, if it will ease your conscience, I intended staying up here with you for a little while — that is, if you don't mind?"

"Of course not," Karen said shyly. ·

Miss Pilbright settled herself in the wicker easy-chair with its blue cushion and there was a little silence that Karen finally broke.

Looking down at the dainty tray with its well-cooked bacon and eggs, she said dreamily:

"No one has ever bothered to do anything as nice as this for me before!"

"As breakfast in bed?" Miss Pilbright smiled. There was something very engaging and childlike about this girl whom

Aubrey assured her was well over twenty-one. Yes, engaging. But rather disconcerting. "Well, I hope you are enjoying it!"

"It's lovely." Karen stroked the edge of the tray cloth with loving fingers. "Did you embroider this?"

"Mercy, no!" Miss Pilbright looked down at her strong, capable hands. "Knitting is my limit! A niece did that for a birthday present. Now, finish up that breakfast."

When it was done, Miss Pilbright took the tray from her and sat down on the edge of the bed.

"My dear, will you tell me a little bit about yourself?" she said gently.

Karen wrinkled her smooth white forehead.

"There isn't very much to tell," she said slowly. "My father died before I was born and my mother when I was born. So I was brought up by an old aunt — she was on my father's side. The Cotton relatives are on my mother's side. I didn't know much about them until Aunt Mary died. I was about fourteen then. They said that they couldn't do with me in any of their homes because they had children of their own, but they would pay towards my education and find me a job when I was ready. So I lived with another aunt — great-aunt, really. And her husband. They — weren't very nice." Her soft lips quivered as she remembered those years when she had been made to feel so humiliated by her dependence on others. They had been nightmare years. Lonely and haunted by the knowledge that she wasn't the same as other girls. Not as clever or as pretty. And not as lovable. Or else, surely, her guardians would have shown her a little affection. "Then, when I finished school, I think they would have liked me to stay on with them because I was quite useful by then. Not with books. I was always bottom of the class. But about the house."

"Yes, I quite expect you were," Miss Pilbright said drily. "Go on."

"But the Cotton relations insisted on them sticking to their bargain. *They* wanted me to look after Miss Cotton. So I did. And that's all."

For a moment Miss Pilbright did not reply. But she thought a lot. The iniquity of it! The poor, unloved little scrap, pushed from pillar to post, taken advantage of, made to feel beholden for every grudging gift! At that moment Miss Pilbright almost offered Karen a home with her and her brother, but — something held her back.

She got up and stood looking out of the window.

"My brother has gone up to Town," she said at length. "He left instructions that you were to have a nice, lazy day. And then, when he comes home this evening, he wants to have a talk with you."

"Yes; about a job," Karen said quickly. "I must get one quickly, you know. I have only the hundred pounds that Miss Cotton left me, and that will soon melt if I start using it!"

"Yes; you should regard that as a nest egg," Miss Pilbright said approvingly. "But as to getting a job at once — we want you to stay with us for a while first. No; don't refuse yet. Wait until after my brother has talked to you. And now, if you feel ready to get up, I will go downstairs. The bathroom is just opposite your door and there is plenty of warm water if you would like a bath."

As she got to the door she turned.

"You know," she said a little uncertainly, "this is not a very exciting house for a young girl like you to live in, but — I — I wish you would stay. You see, I've never had anybody young to look after."

"Dear Miss Pilbright——" Karen began, touched at the feeling in the older woman's voice.

But Miss Pilbright, scared of her own exhibition of emotion, had already closed the door behind her and Karen was left to her own reflections. A bath first thing in the morning! What luxury!

So she luxuriated in the warm, fragrant water — Miss Pilbright had called up that she was to use the bath salts standing on the window ledge, and she had, but rather timidly.

She lay there contentedly, admiring the chromium taps — also a novelty. Brass that required cleaning every day had been her experience. She liked the white tiles, too. They would be easy to keep clean. She wondered if, perhaps, after all, it would be possible to live with the Pilbrights. There would be a lot that she could do to help,

17

but she had the impression that Miss Pilbright was quite capable of running her own house. Still, it would be nice, she thought wistfully. She rather dreaded going to new people. Suppose they were not satisfied with her and were cross. She wondered just what sort of job it was that Mr. Pilbright had in mind for her. Probably something to do with one of his clients — someone old, she expected, like Miss Cotton. Her heart sank a little and suddenly she remembered something else that Mr. Pilbright had suggested. That she might get married. She gave a little shudder. That was the last thing on earth that she wanted. Fancy being absolutely dependent on a man for every single thing you had, of giving up your individuality because money gave him the whip hand and it was what he wanted that mattered. And one would not even have the sanctuary of a shabby room of one's own. One's whole life would have to be shared.

"No!" She was unconscious that she spoke aloud. "I'd rather starve!"

She got hurriedly out of the bath, for the faintly sensual enjoyment of it had suddenly vanished. She dressed hurriedly, brushed her dark hair till it shone with satin smoothness and went slowly downstairs.

She found Miss Pilbright arranging flowers on the big mahogany dining-room table that was protected from the water by a sheet of plastic.

"Ah, my dear, there you are!" she said pleasantly. "Now, how would you like to spend the morning? You are to regard this as a holiday, you know," she went on, forestalling Karen's suggestion that she should help her. "And really, there is nothing for you to do. I have a good woman in from the village every morning, and I thought you might like to have lunch out, so there will be nothing to do until it is time to prepare dinner for this evening."

"I see." Karen's heart sank a little. That seemed to dispose of the possibility that she might stay on with the Pilbrights! "It is country round here, isn't it?" she asked, and Miss Pilbright nodded.

"Not perhaps quite so open as it used to be, but there are still some lovely walks. Would you like to explore?"

"All by myself, do you mean?" Karen's face lit up.

Miss Pilbright looked amused.

"Why not? You're grown up, you know!"

"Yes, I know, but — when I was a child I was never allowed to go out by myself, and since I have been grown up there has never been time to do anything but hurry through the shopping," Karen explained, not self-pityingly, but simply as one stating a fact.

"Then it is quite time you did go out alone," Miss Pilbright said firmly. "Now, listen. When you go out of our gate, turn to the left and that will take you straight into the village. It's considered rather pretty, although I think a cobbled street is a messy and unhygienic affair. It collects dust in the summer and mud in the winter. When you get past the shops, you can keep straight on or branch to the left. The main road is pretty, but flat. The left fork takes you up to Hollow Ponds and the woods. You can't miss your way. Be careful to shut any field gates behind you, that's all."

Karen nodded, her eyes glowing, and she went upstairs to fetch her coat. When she came down, Miss Pilbright looked at her with troubled eyes.

"My dear, haven't you a thicker coat than that? It's autumn, you know, and you've only got a thin dress on."

Karen flushed and fumbled nervously with the button of her thin, shabby coat.

"It's the only one I have," she said apologetically, as if she had been caught out in a fault.

"Oh well, walk briskly," Miss Pilbright suggested. But when she was alone, she clicked her tongue irritably.

"Now, how could I have been so tactless!" she criticised herself angrily. "Poor child, if she had a thicker coat, of course she would have put it on!" She sighed and shook her head. "I don't know——" she meditated. "When Aubrey first told me about this job, I said it was impossible, but — she's destitute and no one cares a rap what happens to her. It would be something for her to have the safety of independence. And it can't last for long."

Dinner was rather a silent meal, because all three people at the table were thinking of what Mr. Pilbright was going to say after dinner. Two of them realised that so much

19

depended on just how he said it. The third was just generally apprehensive.

And when, later, Mr. Pilbright looked at the pale, sensitive face of the girl in front of him, he almost decided not to say anything after all. And then, to his surprise, his sister, who had all along disapproved of the plan, said sharply:

"Well, get along with it, Aubrey! It's only a few hours to bedtime and if you don't get started you'll never get finished!"

So, hesitatingly, he began.

"My dear, would you consider taking on the care of an invalid? Oh, not an elderly person like Miss Cotton," he said hurriedly, seeing the apprehension in Karen's face. "Quite a young person."

"Oh-h!" Karen breathed softly with a pity not for herself but for someone who was young yet ill. "Is she very bad?"

"It isn't a she. It's a he," he said bluntly, while Miss Pilbright clucked disapprovingly in the background at his lack of finesse. "No; don't say anything yet," he went on hurriedly as he saw a refusal shaping on her lips. "Listen to the story first."

Karen sank back into the chair from which she had half got up and made herself listen. Not, of course, that it was any use. How could she possibly nurse a young man? After all, it was not as if she were a trained nurse.

"Until a month ago, Christopher Thirlby was one of the strongest, most athletic young men I have ever met," Mr. Pilbright began precisely. "Tall, handsome, with enough money to live with comfort, and a hobby which seemed to satisfy a need for speed and movement which his rather restless nature demanded. He was a test pilot for a firm of aeroplane designers and makers."

"Oh!" Karen breathed again, her grey eyes wide with horror as she saw to what the story was leading.

"Yes; you are quite right. Something went wrong. I do not know the details. Anyhow, Christopher crashed. It is, everyone agrees, a miracle that he is alive to-day. But" — he placed the tips of his fingers together with a nice precision and shook his head — "it would have been a mercy if he had been killed. After a month of examination of every kind, the specialists have told him that there is nothing that they can do. They say that he will lie there, unable to move, except for one hand, until he dies. And that will be — must be — in six months' time — or sooner. Now do you understand?"

"But, Mr. Pilbright, it isn't possible," Karen said earnestly. "It isn't that I am not terribly sorry for Mr. Thirlby but — I'm not a professional nurse. And, surely, that is what he needs?"

"Certainly," Mr. Pilbright agreed. "Actually, he has a male attendant. But he would not require you to nurse him. What he wants is someone who will be even more than a housekeeper in order that his house may be properly run as he had it run before his accident."

Karen, hunched up in her chair, her elbows on her knees and her chin resting on her clenched fists, looked at him uncomprehendingly.

"More than a housekeeper?" she pondered aloud.

Mr. Pilbright cleared his throat.

"Yes. You see, Christopher feels, possibly with some truth, that any servant, however good, would take advantage of his inability to keep his eye on them. So——"

"But whatever he called me, housekeeper or anything else, I should still be a servant," she pointed out earnestly, "because he would be paying me. Don't you see?"

Mr. Pilbright hesitated for a moment and his sister knew that he was choosing his words with very great care. Only — how *could* you possibly say a thing like this tactfully? And evidently Mr. Pilbright realised that too, for he said precisely:

"You would not be a servant. You would be his wife."

CHAPTER TWO

For a moment Karen stared at him uncomprehendingly. Then she jumped to her feet, almost turning over the heavy chair in her agitation.

"No!" she said shrilly. "No! It isn't possible!"

Mr. Pilbright glanced appealingly at his sister. He knew quite well that he had made a mess of it, but how else could he have explained the situation to the child? Confound it, right from the beginning he had said that it was impossible, but that obstinate young fool — no less obstinate now because he was flat on his back — had insisted that it was perfectly feasible.

"If you get the right girl," he had added.

Well, perhaps he was right. But what type was the right one, he'd like to know. Certainly not this frightened unsophisticated infant.

Eleanor pursed her lips together for a second in a way that her brother knew meant that she was thoroughly vexed with him.

"Karen, sit down," Eleanor said kindly but firmly, and Karen immediately responded to the tone of authority.

"Now listen, my dear," Miss Pilbright went on. "Get one thing firmly into your head. We cannot and do not wish to force you to do this. You are an absolutely free agent. But — we do want you to realise exactly what the situation is."

Karen said nothing, but she seemed to relax slightly as if she were at least partially reassured.

"My brother has not told you everything. First of all, this would not be an ordinary marriage. No one could even dream of a girl marrying a perfect stranger if it were. You would be — a friend and companion, nothing more. You understand?"

Karen nodded silently.

"Even so, Christopher realises that not every girl would tackle such a job. Consequently, he is prepared to be very generous. He will pay you five hundred pounds for the six months of life remaining to him, and when he dies, he will

22

leave you all that he has." She leaned forward and touched Karen's hand. "Do you realise what that means? It means that never, so long as you live, need you work for anybody you don't want to. And — you need never be frightened again."

Karen stared at her incredulously.

"But he couldn't!" she protested. "I mean — don't you see, I might say I would do this and — and make his life an absolute misery! Don't you see? It's too much of a temptation! If he got the wrong girl — and how does he know that I am not?"

Mr. Pilbright tugged at his moustache and thought of Christopher Thirlby's cynical laugh when he had said exactly the same thing:

"But that is what I want — the wrong girl! One that is hard and mercenary — who will do anything for money!"

If he told Karen that, Mr. Pilbright knew that there would not be a single chance that she would marry Christopher. So he said:

"You forget, I am in a position to give you a reference. Look how you cared for Miss Cotton."

Karen flushed.

"You — you don't think I did that just for the sake of the hundred pounds, do you?" she asked painfully, and Mr. Pilbright cursed himself.

"No, my child, I don't," he said flatly. "That is why, from Christopher's point of view, I have no fears if you marry him. It is for you——"

He stopped abruptly because his sister had caught his eye and was cautiously shaking her head. He glanced at Karen and saw that she was deep in thought. He waited in silence, wondering what she was thinking.

Karen could hardly have told them, because there was a picture in her mind rather than a thought that could be expressed in words. A picture of a young man who could not move, who was utterly dependent on other people for everything he needed. A prisoner in his own enforced stillness. And something more than pity welled up in her heart: understanding. For a different reason, she too had been a prisoner for years. She knew the aching humiliation of dependence, the loneliness of isolation. She knew

23

that he must be feeling bitter and resentful, and surely she, rather than anyone else he was likely to meet, could help him. She gave a little sigh.

"I will go and see him," she said quietly. "And if we — we feel we can be friends, I will — do as you ask."

Her sudden capitulation caught the Pilbrights unprepared. They sat staring at her in incredulous silence. Then Mr. Pilbright pulled himself together.

"I'm not sure if that is possible," he said doubtfully. "Christopher instructed me to make all arrangements."

Karen stood up.

"Those are the only terms on which I will even think of it," she said gently and yet with a new, rather touching firmness that suddenly made her seem her full years.

"I'll see what he says," Mr. Pilbright said at length. "In the meantime, you had better run along to bed. You must be tired!"

Karen did as he suggested, not because she was tired, but because she felt that it was utterly impossible to be with other people, however nice, any more just now.

She went slowly to her room and, without switching on the light, went over to the window and quietly opened it. In the distance she could see the lights of one other house, but, apart from that, the night was as dark as it was still. Peaceful. But it struck no answering note in her. Instead, her whole being seemed to ache as she thought of the man she had never seen.

"If I could make him happy, it could be — it shall be — the best six months of his life," she vowed.

As to the money, she had completely forgotten every word about it.

Except for the raven darkness of his hair, he looked like a marble effigy on a tomb, she thought. There was one in Westminster Abbey, she remembered. A young French prince or something. His head rested on a marble pillow and was turned slightly to one side, just as Christopher's was. And on each face was the same half-smile of a man whose dreams are pleasant.

She must have made some slight sound, for his eyes suddenly opened and the illusion was shattered. Brilliant, dominating eyes. The eyes of a man used to command. Somehow they shattered the determination that had been born last night of her pity. This was not a man who would accept sympathy. He would be too proud to admit that he cared what had happened to him — she felt her confidence dwindling. And then his lips parted.

"Who the devil are you?" he asked arrogantly. But, before she could reply, he remembered. "Oh, of course, the girl Pilbright found, Karen — something or other."

"It's — Karenhappuch, really," she said timidly. "And my other name is — Smith."

The information appeared to leave him completely uninterested.

"You seem to think that there is some need for us to see one another before we get married. But I assure you that it is quite unnecessary. There is nothing personal in this marriage. Surely he made that perfectly clear?"

"Oh, but there is," she insisted gravely. "Two people cannot live in the same house without it mattering tremendously if they like one another."

He turned his head away from her.

"I doubt if it matters so much when one of them is a useless log," he said viciously — so viciously that she could guess the agony that lay behind his words.

"I think it might matter even more, then," she said thoughtfully. How dreadful it must be, she thought, to be tied hand and foot so that one could never avoid people—

Perhaps he guessed her thoughts, for he looked at her sharply and muttered something that might have been "Thanks!"

"Oh, I wasn't only thinking of you," she said frankly. "*I* had to know——"

"Yes?" he prompted.

She leaned her elbows on her knees just as she had done the night before and rested her chin in her cupped hands.

"Miss Cotton was kind to me," she said broodingly. "That was the old lady I looked after until she — she——"

"Died," he said harshly. "As I am going to die. Go on."

"Kind — in a way. But her illness had — warped her. She hated almost everybody. You could feel the hatred in the house. And after she was dead and they came to see how much there was for them, it was fuller than ever of hatred. And," she finished abruptly, "I can't bear any more of it. That is why I had to know."

"Know what?" He was watching her intently.

"Whether you would be kind to me and — whether we could share a home that was — good — tranquil. I don't quite know how to say it."

His hand moved restlessly on the smooth bedspread. Only he knew why he had told Pilbright to find a girl who would marry him — though he had an idea that the solicitor had guessed something near the truth. But certainly only he knew just what a revenge he had planned to wreak on another woman through this pale, sensitive girl. And for a moment, his own plan appalled him.

But only for a moment. Something harder, more reckless, overcame the momentary weakness. He had to admit that she was clever, that she had almost deluded him into thinking that she was sincere. And then he remembered Stella. Stella, who had married that fool of a Fred so that she could get the Thirlby money without the bother of marrying a crippled invalid.

Stella — this girl, Karen. What difference was there between them? Out for themselves, first, last and all the time. The only way to keep up with them was by letting them think that they had got the better of you, while all the time you were playing your own game.

So now he said, almost gently:

"I don't think you will have any need to complain of my — generosity to you. And — at the worst, it can only be for about six months."

"Yes," she said in a preoccupied way. "I see."

And that was true. Suddenly, she really did see.

She knew that, at the moment at least, it did not lie within Christopher's power to be kind to anyone. That he was bitter, resentful and self-centred. And desperately unhappy. So desperately that she *had* to marry him because she ached with the desire to bring him tranquility and peace, even for a little while, even at the cost of her own happiness and tranquility.

"If you are quite, quite sure you want me to, I will marry you," she said steadily.

He lifted his head a fraction from the pillow.

"You will?" There was an eagerness, a virility in his voice that made it seem impossible to believe that here was a man who would be tied to his bed for the rest of his days. "Then — do tell Pilbright to go ahead. He will understand. The marriage licence and all that."

Although he had made so slight a movement, he seemed now to sink back on the bed as if he had made a tremendous exertion. His eyes closed and Karen, standing beside him, saw that something like contentment had come into his face. Her heart gave a little throb. She had pleased him, brought him just a little happiness.

The dark eyes opened again.

"Well? What are you waiting for?" he asked sharply.

Karen turned away without a word and the eyes of the helpless man followed her to the door. Yes, really, Pilbright had chosen extraordinarily well in the short time at his disposal. With a little grooming and dressing, the girl would be able to play her part to his satisfaction. He smiled grimly. He was looking forward to seeing Stella's face when she set eyes on — *his wife!*

In the hall of the luxurious nursing-home to which Christopher had been taken, Karen was stopped by the porter.

"Would you like a taxi, madam?" he asked deferentially. She looked, he thought, like a little nursery governess in those shabby clothes, but one never knew. Christopher Thirlby was a name to juggle with, and she had visited him.

Karen hesitated. It seemed an undreamed-of-luxury but Christopher had instilled some of his own sense of urgency into her and she wanted to get to Mr. Pilbright's office as quickly as possible.

"Yes, please." And then, a little fearfully because it was all so unfamiliar: "That is — can you tell me how much it will cost?"

"Depends where you want to go, miss," he said, eyeing her curiously.

"To Lincoln's Inn."

"Oh, from here, perhaps four shillings. Not more. Except——" He hesitated for a moment and then decided that, in spite of her shabbiness, she was a lady and a nice little thing as well. "Look, miss, if you don't mind me telling you, you must tip the driver as well. A shilling or so."

"Oh, thank you," she said gratefully. "You see, I've never been in London before, so it is all unfamiliar."

He smiled encouragingly.

"You'll be all right, miss," and so she would be, he thought. Something about her——

He fetched a taxi for her and handed her in and Karen was completely unaware that the hall porter was smiling, because most people would have tipped him as well and she had not. For some strange reason, instead of this annoying him, he found that he was rather pleased.

She was shown into Mr. Pilbright's office with a celerity that suggested instructions had been given not to waste time when she arrived.

Mr. Pilbright looked up eagerly as she came in, but he could make nothing of her expression. There was something mask-like about it, as if she were hiding a secret, and with a little pang of something like guilt he realised that, in a few hours, she had grown older.

"Well?" he asked.

"May I sit down?" Karen asked and sank gratefully into the chair he hurriedly pulled up for her. She looked at him gravely, and with a new composure of which she was completely unaware. "Christopher says please will you make all the necessary arrangements."

"You — you *are* going to marry him, then?" he said incredulously.

She looked at him wonderingly.

"Oh yes. There was nothing else I could do," she said simply.

His alert eyes seemed to intensify their shrewdness as he watched her. Had he been mistaken? Was she like so many girls — willing to pay any price for the sake of money? He shrugged his shoulders ever so slightly. Well, after all, why not? It was not an easy world for women, and money made all the difference. He had held it out as bait to her. And yet he was disappointed.

"So, will you?" she asked.

He gave himself a little shake and nodded.

"Yes. And I had better explain to you just what it is that Christopher wants done. You may have noticed that there is a church just next to the nursing home?"

"No. I'm afraid I didn't," she confessed. "I — was thinking about other things."

Mr. Pilbright cleared his throat.

"Yes, I suppose so. Well, take my word for it, there is. Now, the law is that you cannot be married out of your own parish unless you spend three weeks as a resident in the parish where you wish to be married. Christopher, by having been in the nursing home for over that period, therefore qualifies."

"How about me?" she asked anxiously.

"Oh, it is only the person who applies for the licence who needs to qualify," he assured her. "I shall act on his behalf, and that will be all right. I shall get a licence by means of which you can be married two days later."

"In that church?" Karen asked quietly.

"In that church. Christopher will be wheeled in on one of the nursing-home trolley-stretchers. That will be quite easy. After, he will be transferred to an ambulance and will be driven straight down to Claverings."

"That is his house?" she asked, and he looked at her thoughtfully. Should he explain to her just what his financial position was? No; on the whole he thought better not. Let her find it out for herself.

"Yes; that is his house. It is in Sussex."

"Oh, I've never been there," Karen said, mildly interested. Then something else concerned her. "There will be room in the ambulance for me as well, won't there?"

"Christopher prefers that you should travel down by car. He thinks it would be more comfortable for you," he said diplomatically. What Christopher had actually said was: "I'm perfectly well aware that this journey is going to knock me out, so the fewer people who see me the better. I'm not cadging for pity."

Karen did not speak immediately, and when she did, it made the old solicitor jump. It was almost as if she had read his thoughts.

"How he must hate people seeing him helpless," she said softly. "A man who has been so strong." She sighed.

"I must remember that. It will mean that he hates anyone showing pity."

They arranged that she should go with him to the register office. Fortunately, it was near to the nursing-home and the Registrar agreed to pay Christopher a visit, since he was unable to come to him.

"Unusual," he commented. "Still, in the circumstances——"

So the licence was procured and taken to the Vicar, who listened in silence to their explanations and then turned to Mr. Pilbright.

"I should like to have a word with this young lady alone, if you do not mind," he said gravely.

Mr. Pilbright hesitated, but had no alternative than to agree. He went out of the room and closed the door behind him, knowing that he had done all that was possible to please his difficult client. The rest must be left to Fate — and the slim, grave little girl who sat now facing the Vicar with her hands folded primly in her lap.

The Vicar looked at her with great kindness.

"My dear, how old are you?"

"Twenty-two," she said promptly.

"I see. And — have you no relatives who are — interested in your future?"

"No. None at all. I have got relations," she explained carefully, "but they are not in the least bit interested in me. You see, they are cross because I inherited some money and they did not get any."

"Oh, so you have independent means!" He sounded relieved. As he was. At least the child was not being forced into this odd marriage because she was in need.

Karen said nothing. She was not quite sure what he meant, but evidently the fact that she had some money made him feel reassured. So that was all right.

"Now, tell me, Miss — Smith, isn't it? Yes — well, tell me, my dear, you have known each other for some time? Or what I should say is, you have — cared for Mr. Thirlby for some time? You are marrying him for love, not for pity."

Karen hesitated. She was sure that this kindly clergyman was only doing what he felt was his duty but she wished that he would not ask questions. It seemed an intrusion into something that was private and her own. She wished that she could have lied to him, but she knew quite well from past experience that she was always found out even in the whitest lie told for sheer self-protection.

"I only met Mr. Thirlby two days ago," she said precisely.

He gave an exclamation of dismayed surprise.

"But, my dear — this is terrible! You do not understand. You are going to take vows to love, honour and cherish a man about whom you know absolutely nothing! You are linking your life to that of a stranger! I am not sure that I should not be right to refuse to perform this ceremony."

"I don't think you understand," she said levelly. "It can't be for all my life. Christopher cannot live long. And, in the meantime, he needs caring for. And I am going to be the one that does it."

"I see." He sighed, and shook his head. "That is reassuring in one sense. Though in another—— Look, Miss Smith, suppose, in that time, you grow to love your husband? What then? You have to face separation in a very short time. Or, on the other hand, suppose a miracle takes place — and such things have been known to happen. Suppose he lives. You will be tied to a man you don't love. Have you thought of that?"

"But then I might fall in love with him and he might live," Karen pointed out. "No one can tell. All I know is this — what I am doing is *right*. Oh please do believe that! Because, if you don't, it will only mean that we have to go to another church farther away from the nursing-home, and that will tire Christopher more."

He hesitated and shook his head doubtfully. Then finally he sighed and said:

"Very well. I will do as you ask. And God forgive me if I am doing wrong!"

"Oh, you're not," Karen promised him earnestly. "I know it!"

So she was able to go back to the nursing-home and tell Christopher that everything was arranged. They would be married that afternoon.

"Good girl!" He spoke more kindly to her than he had done on their first meeting, but she realised that it was only because he was pleased at having got his own way, so it gave her no very personal sense of satisfaction.

"How are you going to spend the time between now and then?" he asked, suddenly apprehensive.

She guessed that he was half-afraid she might back out at the last minute, so she took care to make her voice sound as matter-of-fact as possible.

"I am going to buy a heavier coat than this one," she told him. "Mr. Pilbright suggested that it was the most practical thing to do, because there are not any suitable shops near your home."

He smiled sardonically.

"So you've got Pilbright twisted round your little finger already," he commented. "He made no bones about forwarding you the money?"

"Oh no. I thought it was very kind of him, but he says that there is no doubt about it. I shall get Miss Cotton's hundred pounds, so I can pay him back then."

"Miss Cotton? Who the devil is she? Oh, I remember. The woman you nursed until she — died. Good Lord, do you mean to say——" He broke off, but he seemed to be consumed with some inner laughter as if she had said something really funny. Suddenly he realised that she looked both puzzled and a little hurt and he stopped. "Look here, what is it — Karen? I want you to do something for me. Take a taxi to this address." He fumbled awkwardly under the pillow and produced a letter. "It's a firm of jewellers. Give them the letter and they will give you two rings — your engagement ring and your wedding ring. If they don't fit, wait for them to be altered. It will only take a little while. Understand?"

"Yes," she admitted. "But——"

"What is it?" he said impatiently. "I don't like giving instructions twice."

"I know I've got to have a wedding ring," she said slowly. "But — is there any need for an engagement ring? I mean — it isn't as if you——" She paused and finished lamely: "Isn't it an unnecessary extravagance?"

He looked at her curiously and with a certain cynical

amusement. What a clever little minx she was with her demureness and her pretence that his money did not matter.

"You will do as I ask," he said shortly and saw the sensitive lips quiver. He was shrewd enough to realise that that was a genuine danger signal. Perhaps he was mistaken. He was too tired to concern himself with that. But at least he must make an effort not to scare her off. He needed her. "I'm sorry if I snapped at you," he said, deliberately infusing a gentle note into his voice. "It's so damned infuriating being stuck here, and when people are slow——" He had not meant to say as much as that, but, to his relief, she did not weep over him. She simply nodded her head as if in complete agreement and said feelingly:

"If I were you, I should want to *hit* them. All right. I'll do exactly as you say. And now I'd better hurry or I shall keep you waiting!"

Some little shred of feminine vanity, surprisingly left in her after so many years of other people's made-over clothes, persuaded her to buy the coat first. She hesitated over the colour of it. Should it be black out of respect for Miss Cotton? Then she discarded the idea. Miss Cotton belonged to the past. It was of Christopher that she must think, and he certainly would not want to be surrounded by depressing colours. She looked carefully into a whole string of shops before she decided on a soft powder blue which, she was assured by the assistant who served her, suited her perfectly. It was rather long, according to Karen's ideas, but again the assistant insisted that it was the fashionable length.

"If Madam were to wear slightly higher heels——" she suggested.

Karen looked down at her shabby little shoes and realised that she must do something about them as well, for the new coat showed them up so much. And a hat.

She chose black suède shoes — the prettiest ones she had ever had — and wore both them and the coat when she went in search of a hat. That was more difficult, but in the end she found one that was described as a halo to her unfamiliar ears. It certainly was rather like one, although surely no halo was ever made of deep blue velvet.

Gloves — she had nearly forgotten them, but she did not put them on. They must look absolutely spotless when she went to the church. All the same, she was guilty of the childlike vanity of carrying them carefully in her hand when she went to the jeweller's shop whose name appeared on Christopher's letter. And when she saw the magnificence of the shop, she was thankful that she had. She was tempted to stop and stare at the delightful things displayed in the windows — she had never seen anything like them. But there was also a clock hanging above the shop and it told her that she must not dawdle. So, taking her courage in both hands, she went in and gravely presented Christopher's letter.

They had, perhaps, looked at her a little dubiously as she had come in, but the letter altered all that. A message was sent to someone in a room with so much glass to it that Karen felt its occupant must feel as if he lived in an aquarium, and a suave, immaculately dressed man came out.

He greeted her with such deference as she had never known existed and which, secretly, she found horribly embarrassing, and then, from the deep recesses of a huge safe, he produced a box and opened it.

There were two rings in it. A wedding ring because it was plain, although, to Karen's surprise, it was a whiteish metal instead of the gold to which she was used. And another ring. Her engagement ring,

"A very beautiful stone," the immaculate gentleman said complacently. "We are quite sure that Mr. Thirlby will be delighted with it. And with the setting. Will Madam try it on for size."

Silently, Karen held out her small, work-stained hand. The ring slipped easily over her knuckle and Karen stared at it incredulously. A single stone over a quarter of an inch in diameter and full of what seemed like liquid fire.

"What is it?" Karen asked, too fascinated to mind displaying her ignorance.

"A diamond, madam. A very beautiful diamond," she was told.

"But — it looks likes rubies and sapphires and emeralds all mixed up!" she said breathlessly, completely unaware of the glances that were being exchanged behind her back.

"That is the cutting," the immaculate gentleman explained suavely, contriving to scowl at the amused assistants. If they did not realise that this was the future Mrs. Christopher Thirlby, he did. And he had every intention of retaining her custom. "It catches the light and breaks it up into its component parts, so that you have all the colours of the spectrum displayed as you move the ring."

"I see," Karen said a little doubtfully. It sounded a simple explanation — except that she did not understand a word of it. And in any case, it really hardly mattered. Nothing could explain the sheer magic of this beautiful thing that Christopher was giving her.

"The wedding ring is sure to fit Madam because it is the same size," she was assured.

"Hadn't I better try it on?" she suggested. Christopher would, she felt sure, be furious if it stuck, when she wore it for the first time in the church.

The manager shrugged.

"Most ladies feel that it is unlucky to try on a wedding ring beforehand," he explained. "But if Madam wishes——"

"No!" Karen said sharply. She did not know if she believed in luck or not, but she certainly was not going to do anything that even other people thought was unlucky. "Never mind!"

"You will wear the other?" he suggested and Karen deliberated.

"No," she said slowly. Surely, Christopher would prefer to give it to her himself? Then, suddenly, she changed her mind. "Yes, I will," she said firmly. "It will be safer on my finger than in a box I could lose."

"Quite so, madam." Everything that she did was right — she was the future Mrs. Thirlby. But the manager was something of a cynic. A nice, quiet-looking little thing. Not perhaps what you would expect Mr. Thirlby to have chosen; still, in one thing like all the rest of them. Once she had got her hands on to jewellery, she couldn't bear to let it go even for an odd hour or so!

And Christopher, when he saw it sparkling and twinkling on her finger, thought exactly the same thing.

"Clever — but not quite clever enough," he thought with a feeling almost akin to triumph. Well, at least, he had no need to feel any compunction now. She was evidently quite capable of looking after herself.

There had been another wedding at the church that afternoon. From Christopher's window, Karen had seen the happy bride come out on her husband's arm. They were laughing gaily as they met the barrage of their friends' confetti, and Karen's heart gave a sickening little lurch. That was the way two people who were getting married ought to feel. Not——

"What the deuce is all that row?" Christopher asked fretfully.

"Just — some people passing by," Karen said steadily.

And then, it was time for Christopher to be lifted on to the light steel trolley. Silently Karen followed behind him into the lift that was deep enough to take the trolley and several people as well.

In the hall, Mr. Pilbright and his sister were waiting. They both looked grave, and so did the nurse who accompanied them — though her eyes were on the flushed face of her patient.

The floral decorations from the previous wedding were still in the church, and although Karen knew that they had not been put there for her, they gave the rather gaunt church a friendly air. And somebody put a bouquet into her hands as she walked up the nave. Silently the trolley was wheeled up to the chancel steps and the service began. Vaguely, Karen was conscious of Mr. Pilbright standing on her left, of Miss Pilbright relieving her of the bouquet, and a small group of other people behind her. But they were of little account. Christopher, chalky white now, lying motionless beside her, held all her attention. What was he feeling, she wondered? And why was he marrying her?

Mechanically, she made her responses, listened to his. And it was all over. Registers were signed. She took her flowers again and walked down the aisle beside Christopher. His eyes were closed now and he looked utterly exhausted.

She waited while he was transferred to the ambulance. Then she turned to the car that had drawn up at a little distance. Even her inexperienced eyes told her that it was

36

an expensive one, and she glanced for reassurance at Mr. Pilbright.

"Yes; this is for you," he said in a matter-of-fact tone. "One of Christopher's. He ordered it up for you."

"Oh," she said a little breathlessly. "That was kind of him," and stood back for Miss Pilbright to get in first. But Mr. Pilbright was holding out his hand, and suddenly she realised that she was to go alone. So she shook hands and thanked them for all that they had done, refusing to take any notice of the sudden panic that surged through her.

Then she got into the big car. Mrs. Christopher Thirlby off on her honeymoon, complete with a bouquet, a wedding ring and an engagement ring.

And a husband too, of course. But he preferred not to have her with him more than he could help.

Then why, why, *why* had he married her?

CHAPTER THREE

THE warmth of the day went early and Karen was glad of the thick coat she had bought. Even so, she shivered now and again, and more than once she looked longingly at the thick, furry rug that lay beside her on the seat, but it was some time before she could feel that she had any right to touch it. When at last she did, its pleasant warmth made her drowsy and at last she slept from sheer nervous exhaustion.

It was not until the car stopped that she awoke with a jerk and realised that they had pulled up in front of a house. She peered out of the window, but the daylight had failed and she was only able to see the dim outline of the building. Then the door opened and a flood of light shone out. Instinctively she smoothed back her silky hair with a nervous gesture and then the car door opened.

"This is Claverings, madam," the chauffeur told her. He turned back the rug so that she could get out and Karen shivered, though less with the chill of the evening air than with apprehension.

And it was well-founded apprehension. Perhaps the magnificent ring on her finger and the luxurious car ought to have prepared her but the fact remained that she had simply not given any consideration to the probable size of Christopher's house. And now, to her troubled eyes, it appeared to be an absolute mansion. With sudden panic, she realised that it was the sort of house where there would be superior servants — butlers and housekeepers. And they would be quick to realise that she was not used to such surroundings. That meant that they would despise her, which would annoy Christopher, and he would be cross with her.

She set her teeth. That just must not happen. For herself she could not find the courage, but for Christopher's sake — that was another matter.

She walked resolutely into the warm, well-lit hall. To her relief, there was only one elderly woman, who advanced smilingly towards her.

"Good evening, Madam," she said pleasantly. "I am Mrs. Paynton, the housekeeper."

"Good evening, Mrs. Paynton," Karen said gravely, and then, seeing the big fire roaring in the square stone grate she exclaimed impulsively: "Oh, how lovely!"

"The evenings are chilly now. We only use logs, but I thought it would be — something of a welcome to you, Madam."

Karen heard the brief hesitation and for a moment her eyes dropped. So even the servants realised the oddness of her marriage and were sorry for her. Then she realised that there had been real kindness in the thought and she smiled at the housekeeper as she walked over to the welcome warmth.

"How very kind of you," she said, forcing back the silly tears that would come to her eyes.

The housekeeper indicated a little table on which a covered dish, a glass and a decanter were set.

"Would you care for a little refreshment before you see your room, madam?" she asked.

Karen caught her breath. Surely this was more than one expected a housekeeper to do without instructions.

"Did — Mr. Thirlby have this put here for me?" she asked eagerly.

Mrs. Paynton's eyes avoided hers.

"Not directly, madam," she hedged. "But it is the custom of the house that there shall always be a little something ready for any guests who have travelled any distance. Of course, you are not a guest, madam," she added hastily. "But — I thought——"

"It was very kind of you," Karen said mechanically. "I should like—— But first of all, where is Mr. Thirlby? I lost sight of his ambulance."

"He arrived about half an hour ago, madam," she was told. "And went straight to his room. His man, Bannister, is looking after him. I was to tell you that he hoped everything would be to your liking, but he was feeling too tired this evening to see anyone. He said that he was sure you would quite understand."

Mrs. Paynton looked anxiously at the slim, pale girl who stood staring into the fire. She was a kindly, conscientious woman who had been with the Thirlbys ever since Christopher's boyhood, and with pursed lips she put this down as just one more of Master Christopher's tricks. There had been some in the past that had borne pretty serious fruit, but this one seemed to her to have more dangerous possibilities to it than anything that had gone before.

"Yes, of course," Karen said slowly, unaware of the housekeeper's anxious eyes. She gave herself a resolute little shake and accepted the glass of sherry from the housekeeper and helped herself to a perfectly cut sandwich. The wine warmed her and to some extent heartened her.

"I would like to see my room now," she said to Mrs. Paynton, who had quietly withdrawn to the back of the hall until she was required.

She turned and crossed to the staircase and as she did so, a small kitten dashed out from some hiding-place and nearly tripped her up.

"Oh, you darling!" she said impulsively and picked the scrap up. With the engaging friendliness of kittens, he snuggled up against her, purring like a small dynamo.

Mrs. Paynton clicked her tongue.

"I can't keep him in the kitchen," she apologised. "Now, his old mother knows her place exactly, but this one is that venturesome. Now, come here, you naughty thing!"

But Karen hugged the warm little body.

"Oh, please, let me keep him," she begged, completely forgetting that she was the mistress of this house and consequently of all that was in it. "He's so sweet and — homely."

"Oh but of course, madam," the housekeeper said a little doubtfully. "The only thing is the dogs——"

"What sort of dogs?" Karen asked quickly.

"Oh — a retriever and an Airedale, madam. The master's constant companions."

"That will be all right," Karen said confidently. "Big dogs don't mind cats. It's terriers that dislike them so much. And the kitten will soon learn to leave them alone."

"Yes, madam," Mrs. Paynton assented tonelessly. "This is your room."

She flung open a door and Karen caught her breath. The hall and the staircase had been magnificent, but they were, in a sense, impersonal and they had not prepared her for the degree of luxury and comfort that this room held — her room.

She went slowly in and, to her relief, heard the door close gently behind her.

She had thought Miss Pilbright's spare room a haven of comfort, but this——

Her feet sank into a carpet that felt inches deep and was a soft blend of greens and cream. The furniture, she realised, was old, though of a very different oldness from Miss Cotton's Victorian monstrosities. It was, in fact, Chippendale walnut made even more lovely by the years of polishing that it had received. There was nothing old, though, about the deep-sprung mattress and the puffy green eiderdown, but the sheets, when she came to look closer, were fine linen worn to the softness of silk.

There was an electric fire burning and in front of it a couch. That seemed a little odd, Karen thought. After all, if you wanted to rest, there was the bed. Still, it was a relief to sit down, and the kitten, sleepy now with the sudden tiredness of young things, curled up tightly in her lap.

And Karen sat very still in the beautiful room. Suddenly she had realised just what she had done.

She had simply exchanged one prison for another. Oh, that might sound silly when she was surrounded with every comfort, and, for the first time in her life, was evidently going to have more leisure than she had ever known, but it was the truth.

A prison — that Christopher had created about her with his wealth and his indifference. He had spoken of her running his house, but she knew that was absurd. If Mrs. Paynton were a fair example of his servants, they needed no more supervision than they had ever done. So she was barred from filling her time with activities that would at least have been useful. He had no desire, she realised, for her company. Why should he? They were strangers. The fact that she, if not he, needed human companionship simply did not enter into it. So his indifference put up barriers that condemned her to loneliness.

No, the fact of it was that, whatever the Pilbrights might say, she was nothing more than a servant. A well-paid one,

41

but nothing more. A real wife would have had obligations and privileges. She had neither. She could no more go to Christopher's room when he had said he did not want her than the meanest scullery-maid in his employ. She must wait until she was sent for — and then she would have no choice but to obey.

She turned her head into the soft cushions and wept, softly, heartbrokenly.

Her wedding night! And here was she, alone, desperately needing reassurance, and somewhere else in this beautiful house was the man she had married, lonely, too. And suffering. And there was absolutely nothing that she could do about it.

A soft, white mist pressed against the windows when Karen awoke, but gradually dwindled as the sun became more energetic. She put on her thin kimono and tiptoed over to the window. She gasped a little at what she saw. Even so late in the year, there was an exquisite garden full, it seemed to her, of flowers. Mostly chrysanthemums, but a blaze of colour none the less. There was a glimpse of water, too. She was not sure whether it was a pond or a river, but it sparkled agreeably and was a distinct addition to the view. But what startled her was the extent of the land that was obviously attached to the house. You simply could not see its limits.

"At least," she thought wryly, "it is quite a *big* prison!"

She had discovered the night before that there was a bathroom attached to her room; so now she bathed and dressed. There was a discreet tap at the door and a maid came in.

"Oh — I didn't think you would be ready for your tea any earlier, madam!" she said with evident dismay.

Karen smiled reassuringly. The girl was younger than she and evidently more than a little bit scared of her new mistress.

"One rarely sleeps well in a strange bed," she said. "So I got up. But I shall enjoy the tea just as much now!"

"Shall I ask cook to put your breakfast forward, miss — madam, I mean?" the girl suggested. "It was to have been at nine."

"No — yes, please do," Karen said firmly. She had been quick to realise that she had started the day too soon — that if she had breakfast early it would mean a long, dragging morning, and that had prompted an instinctive refusal. But then, Christopher might want her, so the sooner she was through with it the better.

Only, he did not want her. He did not send for her all that day. Or the next. Or the one after that. And Karen could stand it no more.

She had quickly discovered where Christopher's rooms were. The house was an old Tudor manor built in the shape of an "E" with the centre stroke omitted. Her own room was in one of the wings thus formed, with the sitting-room that was evidently intended for her special use under it. Christopher's two rooms were on the ground floor of the other wing, so that he could be wheeled from one to the other without difficulty.

The servants were well-trained and attentive. Her meals were beautifully served, any small wish that she expressed faithfully carried out. Mrs. Paynton visited her every morning, followed by Cook, but both visits were purely perfunctory. Each woman knew her work inside and out and there was nothing for Karen to do but say, "That will be very nice!" It was, she thought, a singularly uninteresting way of housekeeping.

She could feel them all wondering what she was doing here, why Christopher had married her — and small wonder. Didn't she spend half her time wondering that as well?

It was an intolerable position and one which, she told herself critically, would never have happened if she were not such a coward.

But in three days, sheer desperation overcame cowardice. She had explored the house, gone for walks in the garden, tried to read — and she had come to the end of her tether. Immediately after breakfast on the fourth day, she went to the other side of the house and met Bannister, Christopher's man, coming out of his room.

"Good morning, Bannister," she said gravely. "How is Mr. Thirlby this morning?"

"Oh — quite well, madam." The man sounded startled.

43

"I mean, as well as one can expect. He slept fairly well."

"Good!" Karen said with a calmness that she was far from feeling. "Then it will not tire him too much to see me!"

"But, madam——" Bannister tried to slip his short, stocky figure between her and the door. "Mr. Christopher gave explicit directions——"

"I know," she smiled, sorry for his obvious embarrassment. "But — you see, I have had quite a lot to do with caring for invalids and I know — as I expect you do — that one cannot always permit them to have the last word! Besides" — she flashed him that brief, mischievous smile that had so disconcerted Mr. Pilbright — "how are you going to stop me — short of using physical violence?"

"Well — there's that, madam," he admitted. "And," in a burst of confidence, "I don't say you aren't right. Mr. Christopher ought not to lie there just thinking, thinking all the time. I — I'm not sure it wouldn't be better for him to get downright angry with someone than just turn in on himself like he is doing."

Involuntarily, Karen shivered. She had not found it difficult to realise that Christopher was the sort of person who was used to giving orders and having other people carry them out unquestioningly. But he had never been married before — at least, she supposed he hadn't. And it meant obligations. It had to. Even though he was an invalid.

She went quietly into the room. It was furnished exactly like an ordinary sitting-room, except that, where one might have expected to find a couch, there was an invalid's day bed. He did not turn his head when she came in, evidently assuming that it was Bannister returning. She waited for a moment, watching him. His head was turned away from her and he was gazing through the open french window into the garden beyond. With a little stab of pain, she wondered what he was thinking of, what he was regretting, and unconsciously she sighed.

He looked towards her instantly.

"How long have you been there?" he asked sharply.

"I've just come in," she said quietly.

His dark, heavy brows met in a frown.

"I hate being stared at," and the angry resentment in his tone spoke volumes.

"Yes; so do I." Karen agreed. "It makes one feel horribly self-conscious."

He looked at her suspiciously. Was she just being the complete innocent as part of her act, or did she realise that to put his own hideous self-consciousness for his helplessness on a level with the ordinary dislike that any rather sensitive person has for being stared at was an extremely tactful and clever move?

"What do you want?" he asked curtly.

"To talk things over with you."

He made a little gesture of dismissal with his active hand.

"When I want you, I will send for you," he told her.

"No," she contradicted gently but firmly. "That will not do. I am not your servant, Christopher. I am your wife."

His mouth twisted into the mockery of a smile.

"So you are," he said sardonically. "Well, what is it that you want to say?"

"I want to ask you some questions," she told him, her heart thumping with trepidation.

"Go on," he said shortly. "And sit down," he added.

"You married me three — four days ago," she pointed out, cautiously crossing her fingers for luck as they lay in her lap. "Since then you have refused to see me. Is it unreasonable for me to want to know why?"

He frowned irritably. Her quiet directness disconcerted him. He would have known how to deal with a woman who stormed at him or even one in tears but — not this quiet dignity. He found it difficult to tell her that the truth of the matter was simply that he had seen no particular reason why he should see her. He had married her for one reason only and, as yet, he was not ready to tell her what that was. He frowned as he tried to decide what he should say to her and, not unnaturally, Karen misunderstood.

"Please don't think that I want to force my company on you," she said earnestly. "In any circumstances, that would be hateful — but I do understand what it means when you have to put up with people being with you when you would much rather be alone. You have to, you know, when you are poor and they employ you. So——" She smiled rather uncertainly and repeated: "I do understand, because I couldn't run away any more than you."

He still found nothing to say. Of course, it was all nonsense. She could not understand. The cases were not really parallel at all. And, in any case, she could not know that secret, inner urge for solitude that had possessed him from time to time. People who did not understand had said that he, a rich man, was a fool to take on such a risky job as he had done. They didn't understand. It was the solitude, the fierce delight of knowing that his life depended to a large extent on his own skill.

After a little pause, Karen went on:

"You see, quite apart from anything else, it makes it very difficult for me to be the mistress of your home if the servants know that there is something — odd about our marriage."

He looked at her sharply.

"Have they been uncivil?" he demanded. "Because if so——"

"Oh no, not that," she said quickly. "They have been everything that is kind and considerate."

"Then — what?"

She pursed her lips.

"It isn't very easy to put into words but — because they are such very good servants, they have taken tremendous pains not to embarrass me. I mean, Mrs. Paynton and Cook consult me every morning just as if — just as if I were an ordinary wife, but——"

He should have foreseen that, and he was angry with himself for not having done so. Still, it could be put right.

"Naturally, the drive down here tired me," he said shortly. "But from now on I shall be glad if you will come and see me every morning and every evening." Heaven knew what they would talk about, he thought grimly, but to the end of time the conventions must be observed.

"Is there anything else?" he asked, fighting to keep the weary note out of his voice. He — bored! He — who had never found the days long enough to crowd in all that he wanted to do! Six months stretched forward as if it were eternity.

"Yes. Just one thing." Her fingers automatically crossed

46

once more. "Please, Christopher, why did you marry me?"

Yes, of course, she was bound to ask that sooner or later.

"To be the mistress of my home," he said shortly. "To see that it is run properly now that I am tied to this blasted bed."

Secretly she thrilled that he had revealed his feelings to that extent. If only he would not try to keep up appearances with her — would ease some of his agony by sharing it with her instead of "turning in on himself," as Bannister had put it! But that was something that must be left for the time being. In the meantime——

"Your home would be properly run if neither you nor I were here for years on end," she said positively. "You have the nearest thing to perfect servants that anyone could have. There is nothing for me to do except play at housekeeping."

It was perfectly true and he could find nothing to say. Odd — and confoundedly irritating how often this girl put him in that position.

"So — why——?" she asked helplessly, and added childishly: "Please?"

There was nothing for it. He would have to tell her — well, part of the story, anyhow.

He began to speak slowly, deliberately, even ponderously, so that she knew right from the beginning that there was no possible appeal from anything he might say.

"When I heard the doctor's verdict, I did a lot of thinking. Anyone would. Six months to be got through somehow knowing that there is nothing beyond that."

"But there is——" she began earnestly.

"Is there?" he said indifferently. "I don't know. I'm not sure that I want to know. At any rate, there is nothing familiar, nothing tangible. So I decided that there was only one thing for it. I must live out my life on familiar lines — live it to the full. Entertain — even go about as far as is possible." The fine lines of his mouth twitched and she gave a little cry of distress.

"But it will make you terribly tired," she protested.

"In that case, perhaps I shall sleep at night," he said savagely. "Or I might even shorten the time——" He broke off, biting his lip.

Karen's hands clenched so that the nails bit into her palms. She wanted to put her arms round him, to comfort him — and he didn't want her, could take no comfort from her unless——

"That is what you want to do — most of all?" she said very quietly so that he should not guess the storm of emotion that gripped her.

"Yes," he said curtly.

"Then — we must think out the best ways to make it practicable," she said steadily. Yes, of course, she would do anything that he wanted but — had he realised just what it would mean? If he entertained his old friends, he would see them doing all the things that he could no longer do. Just to see other people walking across a room must be torture.

"Good girl," he said. There was both approval and excitement in his voice, and with a little thrill she realised that she had broken down at least one barrier that he had erected between them. He wanted her to help him. None the less, his next words disconcerted her. He said abruptly: "You will need new clothes — and jewellery."

"No!" she said breathlessly. "No!"

"Yes!" he said arrogantly. "You forget you are my wife. You must look the part." His lips twisted again into that cynical smile that already she had grown to hate. "Most girls would jump at the chance!" he assured her.

"That is why," she began and stopped. "Very well, if that is what you want me to do."

"It is."

She frowned for a moment as she concentrated on a new problem.

"You will have to help me," she said at last. "You see, I don't know anything about the sort of dresses that go with a house like this."

"You'll soon learn," he told her. "In the meantime, go to that desk over there. It isn't locked. That's right. Now, in that small drawer to the left, you'll find a bunch of keys. Bring them to me."

He selected one from the rest and pointed to the small safe on the opposite side of the room.

"Open that," he ordered. "There's a cash-box with a key

marked 'Safe Deposit' in it — and my will, if it interests you — as it should."

She ignored that and brought the key to him.

"You are to go up to Town in the car," he instructed her. "First of all you are to go to an address that I will give you and order clothes. No; tell Madame Zelia who you are and give her *carte blanche* to dress you properly. Never mind how much it costs; it hasn't got to come out of your five hundred pounds. And then," he went on eagerly, ignoring her little cry of protest, "you are to go to the safe deposit. I will give you a letter authorising you to take out all my mother's jewellery. Some of the jewellery is old-fashioned and will have to be reset, but there ought to be something that you can take over immediately. Her pearls. And that reminds me. You are to take Bannister with you. There must be a good many thousand pounds' worth of stuff there, and I've no desire to lose it."

"Surely the chauffeur would be strong enough to keep me from running off with it," she said with the first note of bitterness in her voice that she had allowed to show.

He looked at her in genuine amazement.

"You little fool. I wasn't thinking of anything like that," he said irritably. "Supposing you were spotted leaving the place by someone who was sharp enough to see the possibilities of the situation. No; I'd feel more comfortable if you had two men with you. Actually, it isn't a job for a girl, but there is not anyone else that I can trust."

Her heart gave a wild leap of delight. So he *did* trust her! She was suddenly happier than she had ever thought possible when she had entered the room.

"When shall I go?" she asked.

But suddenly he had lost interest; she guessed that he was tired.

"Oh — to-morrow," he said indifferently. "Anything else?"

She came and stood close beside him.

"Christopher — are they really sure?"

"Who?" he asked vaguely.

"The doctors." She saw his nostrils flare and knew that he was angry, but she had to know. "They can make mistakes, you know," she said desperately.

"Oh, sure they can," he agreed. "One — or even two doctors. But not five."

"Oh-h!" She could not repress the long-drawn sigh of distress. Then she pulled herself together. "I don't know. Even five might. I'd never stop trying."

"So I felt at first. One soon gets over it," he assured her indifferently. He hesitated. "As a matter of fact, there was a sixth."

"And he said something different?" she said eagerly. "More encouraging?"

"That depends on how you look at it," he said judicially. "He agreed that there was nothing to be done except — wait for a miracle. He seemed to think that Nature might step in where surgery can't. I wish to God he'd kept his mouth shut!" he finished savagely. He shut his eyes tightly, and it was obviously a dismissal. She walked over to the door and suddenly he shouted:

"And for heaven's sake, don't tiptoe about the place! It's infuriating!"

Karen turned, two scarlet spots flaming in her cheeks.

"I wasn't!" she said indignantly. "Nobody could make a *sound* on a carpet as thick as this! And if you take the trouble to think about it, you'll know that is true!"

And she slammed the door after her.

Once outside, she leaned weakly against the door.

"Goodness! I didn't know I had such a temper," she told herself.

In the evening, she changed into her best dress and went to see Christopher again.

He was reading when she went in, but he laid the book down on the coverlet. She sat down in a chair facing him and then he saw that she was carrying a little bag.

"What's that?" he demanded, less because he was interested than because it was something to say.

"Some embroidery." She pulled it out for him to see. "I found it in a drawer in my room and I wondered if you would mind me finishing it."

"Now who the devil——" he ruminated. "Certainly not my mother. I doubt if she even knew how to sew a button on, let alone embroider. Can you do work like that?"

"Oh yes — if I have time. The nuns taught me at the convent where I was educated. It's very lovely colouring, isn't it?"

He glanced at the brilliant blues and green that were blended to an exquisite imitation of peacock's feather, and suddenly his face grew animated.

"Take that with you to Madam Zelia," he ordered — it was, she thought, essentially Christopher that he *ordered*, never asked. "Tell her to make it the keynote of most of your clothes. For the rest" — his fingers fumbled among the soft skeins until he had found a deep crimson and a flaming orange — "these!"

"But I should look terrible!" she laughed, thinking that he was not serious. "I never wear bright colours!"

"You heard what I said," he said coldly and she realised that he *was* quite serious.

"Very well, Christopher." Her eyes were on the work that lay in her lap and her voice was subdued and docile. It should have pleased him that he had mastered the mild degree of revolt that she had shown, but it did nothing of the sort. Instead, it irritated him.

He returned, rather ostentatiously, to his book and, after a moment, Karen began to select the silks she needed.

It was very lovely work and she soon became immersed in it, and Christopher, glancing up, was able to study her face for the first time.

The light from his bedside lamp shone on her raven-wing hair and made a sort of radiant nimbus round it. His lips curved sardonically. A saint? Hardly! She was a woman! But, he had to admit, quite an attractive one. Her features were good, her mouth was rather on the generous side, but quite a good shape. A bit too thin, though. He wondered if all the hard-luck tales he had heard about her were true.

She glanced up and caught him looking at her. A soft blush stained the whiteness of her cheeks and a query came into her grey eyes.

"I was wondering——" he stammered. "How do you like my house?"

She laid down her work and with a very thoughtful look in her eyes, gave him all her attention — a pretty trick that would be, he thought, if he were a whole man.

"It is very lovely," she said, but though the words were satisfactory, he took exception to her tone.

"You don't sound exactly convinced," he commented. "Come on. What's wrong with it?"

She hesitated for a moment, then she said:

"It's cold."

"Cold? Then, confound it, order more fires to be lit! We've tons of logs!"

"Oh, not that sort of coldness," she disclaimed. "What I meant was — I think it is a long time since people who loved each other lived here, isn't it?"

He stared at her in astonishment.

"How the devil did you know that?" he demanded.

She shook her head.

"I don't know. But it's true."

"Yes," he admitted unwillingly. "My father and mother — quarrelled like cat and dog. I remember when I was a kid——" he broke off. "Never mind that. Do you like music?"

"I don't really know," she confessed. "I've heard so little. But I like it to *say* something. I heard a tune once — Miss Cotton would not have a wireless, but I heard it one day last summer. Shall I whistle it to you?"

Involuntarily, he laughed.

"Who on earth taught you to whistle?"

Instantly her own joyous laugh bubbled up in response.

"I heard the grocer's boy — and I imitated him. At first I only *blew* — but it came at last."

"Go on!"

Rather shyly, she pursed her lips — and for the first time he realised that she wore no lipstick. True and clear as a bird with liquid notes, she whistled the air she had heard — and suddenly stopped.

"That's all I remember," she said apologetically.

" 'Sheep may safely graze,' " he told her. "It's by Bach. You can get a recording of it when you are in Town if you like."

"Oh — yes, that would be nice," she said contentedly and returned to her needlework.

But Christopher found that he could no longer concentrate on his book. For the first time he began really seriously to consider the girl whom he had married.

Just what was she, with her unexpected good taste, her beautiful laugh and her little saint-like face? Was she what she appeared to be?

CHAPTER FOUR

KAREN's first impression when she reached Madame Zelia's establishment was that Cullen, the chauffeur, had made a mistake.

"But this is a private house," she objected.

"It is quite correct, madam," Cullen assured her. And then, to convince her: "I have been here before."

"Oh," Karen said, and for some reason or other, did not feel in the least bit reassured — though for a very different reason.

She was received by a very smart maid, which added to the illusion of it being a private house, but from there on it was obvious that, in spite of the elegance and charm of the place, these were business premises.

Everything — walls, curtains and floor coverings — was of the softest shade of grey. Half a dozen chairs were arranged in a curve halfway up the long room, and at the far end was a little stage with curtains arranged as wings on either side of it. The only other furniture was a desk at which a tall, dark woman was seated.

She stood up when Karen came in, smiled welcomingly.

"Good morning, Mrs. Thirlby," she greeted her. "I am Madame Zelia."

"Good morning," Karen said shyly.

Oh, if only she could turn tail and run, she thought desperately.

But Madame Zelia was a woman of experience. She knew Christopher and she had a good idea of his social position. One glance at this girl told her that Karen was completely unused to such surroundings as were everyday conditions for him. But it also told her something else. The girl had genuine refinement; her voice was soft and sweet. Her appearance — Madame Zelia was puzzled. Karen reminded her of someone, but for the life of her she could not think who it was. A vague likeness, but still unmistakable. Never mind. It would come back. She would remember.

"Now, I understand that you are paying me the compliment of choosing your trousseau for you," she said pleasantly, motioning Karen to a chair beside her desk. "But that does not altogether suit me. In order to do me the greatest credit, you must wear clothes in which you feel yourself. Do you understand?"

"Yes," Karen agreed, and flashed a sudden smile at Madame Zelia. She had no idea of the surprising effect that the smile had on Madame Zelia.

"Good heavens!" she told herself self-reproachfully. "The girl is *beautiful!* How in the world did I miss it?"

Karen was fumbling in her bag for the skeins of silk that Christopher had picked out.

"My husband — and I — thought that these might serve as some sort of guide," she said, laying them on the polished desk.

Madame Zelia took them up in her hand and regarded first them and then Karen reflectively. She would have gambled all that she had that this quiet, almost drab little girl had never contemplated wearing startling colours like these of her own free will. No; this was Christopher's choice. And, suddenly, she remembered.

Another girl, dark, tall, sophisticated, parading in this very room in a peacock blue evening gown, a scarlet-trousered cocktail suit — and Christopher watching, smiling, admiring.

"Good heavens!" she said weakly to herself and realised that her new client was gazing at her in anxious surprise. She pulled herself together with an effort. That there was something behind all this she did not for a moment doubt, but just what it was she had no time to puzzle out just now. No; the far greater problem was how to use such vigorous colours as these so that they enhanced Karen's delicacy and grace without obliterating it.

"Yes," she mused. "You can wear colours like this to great advantage — but only if the styles are simple. And so long as they are not overdone." In her mind's eye, she translated the blatant scarlet into a warm crimson — or, better still, that unusual reddish brown of that length of cashmere she had wondered how to use. And nothing like pant suits for this girl. Long, sweeping skirts, feminine, graceful. She half closed her eyes and then, with a frankness that was unusual in her, she said suddenly; "I am going to enjoy this. I hope you are, too. And I promise you that I will not make you feel either conspicuous or awkward. Does that reassure you?"

Karen drew a deep breath. She seemed to understand. And if she could keep her word, that would be wonderful. She smiled her gratitude and Madame Zelia nodded. This was to be a job after her own heart. She had to do more than dress the girl. She had to give her clothes that gave her confidence.

"And then — that other — she will look common, a nobody beside her," she thought with some satisfaction. The girl whom Karen resembled had treated her to more than one unpleasant display of temperament.

The visit to the safe deposit was a simple and straightforward business compared with that to Madame Zelia. A dozen or so leather cases were packed into the handsome small suitcase that Bannister had produced — one of Christopher's evidently. Karen signed the necessary receipts and they were off on their return journey to Claverings.

For a brief moment she had considered the possibility of paying a short visit to Miss Pilbright, but regretfully she decided that the visit must be postponed until a later date, when Bannister was able to stay with Christopher. Bannister, she had discovered, had been Christopher's valet for a good many years; but, at an earlier date, he had been a male nurse, and so his care of Christopher had a professional skill.

Mrs. Paynton, crossing the hall, stopped and came to her.

"Oh, madam, I was to tell you that Mr. Christopher wants to see you as soon as you come in!"

"Yes, of course. I will go at once," Karen said and turned, eager-footed, in the direction of Christopher's room.

He was staring out of the window, but he turned his head as she came in.

"You wanted me, Christopher?" she said eagerly.

His eyes wandered over her, cold, appraising.

"Yes; I wanted to see you," he admitted. "But I could

have waited until you had made yourself tolerably tidy!"

He saw her flinch and was savagely glad of it. Somehow the day had been a particularly trying one. He hated everything in the world. His own maimed body, his servants who could do all the things that he would never do again. And above all, this girl.

"I am sorry, Christopher," she said gently. "But, you see, I thought when you said 'at once' you meant — just that!"

So he did. If she had waited to brush her hair and wash her face, he would have been annoyed because she had not obeyed him literally. He scowled because she had read his mood and made a slight movement that was the ghost of a shrug.

"Well, never mind. Show me the stuff you have brought."

Obediently, she called to Bannister, who was waiting in the hall, to bring in the case; and then, one by one, she took out the leather cases, laid them on the table by his bed and opened them. Milky pearls, diamonds, rubies, sapphires, emeralds.

Karen gazed at them in amazement. To her it looked like the entire contents of a jeweller's shop.

"Well?" Christopher asked, his voice faintly amused.

Karen shook her head.

"They are very, very lovely," she said gravely. "But — I do not see how anyone could enjoy wearing them."

"You don't?" His lips curved sardonically. "And why not?"

"They are valuable, aren't they?" she asked.

"Very," he admitted. "The pearls alone are worth several thousand pounds. The diamonds are very good, too, and this ruby alone——"

"That's just it," she said eagerly. "Fancy wearing thousands and thousands of pounds worth of jewels! It would be too much responsibility! Besides——" She stopped, realising that it would probably annoy him to hear her say that to her eyes there was something in rather bad taste about the flashing display that lay between them.

But though she did not put her thought into words, she was disconcerted to find that he had guessed what was in her mind, for he said grimly:

"None the less, you are going to wear them! Put them on now!"

For a moment their eyes met and clashed in conflict, then Karen's dropped and she obeyed his directions as he fumbled in first one case and then another.

"Now go and look at yourself in the glass!" he ordered, watching her closely.

Obediently, Karen went over to the long mirror and stood in front of it. Unwillingly she lifted her eyes to her reflection and as quickly dropped them again.

"You don't like them?" he said in what was quite evidently genuine amazement. "But, my dear girl, most women——"

She turned away from the glass, her soft mouth quivering.

"But I'm not 'most women,'" she protested, her voice almost out of control. "I'm — I'm — myself and I — I——" She shook her head, because the lump in her throat would not let her go on and, with fumbling fingers, she hurriedly took off the lovely things and laid them in a glittering pile on his bed. Then, with her fingers pressed to her quivering lips, she ran out of the room.

For a moment Christopher lay perfectly still. Then, his face mask-like, he rang the little electric bell that lay within easy reach of his hand. When Bannister came in his master was lying with closed eyes.

"Put these damned things away in the safe," he said without expression. "All except the pearls. And be quick, man!" he added impatiently.

Karen came to his room the next morning with an atmosphere of serenity about her that gave no indication of the tears she had shed and the sleepless night she had spent.

Just what she had expected out of this strange marriage of hers she hardly knew. That it would mean sacrifice on her part she had realised, but Christopher's need had seemed to her so great. And now she knew that she would never be of use to him in the way in which she had visualised. He had no desire for her companionship, no interest whatever in her happiness.

And yet, according to his rights, and the unusual proposal he had made to her, he was acting quite fairly to her.

She remembered his exact choice of words:

"I don't think you will have any need to complain of my — generosity to you."

Beautiful clothes, jewellery, the comfort of a luxurious home — yes, she supposed most people would say that he was generous. And yet she knew quite well that she would give all that for a little kindness, a little companionship. And those he was simply unable to give her.

With desperate relief, she seized hold of the word. Unable! She must never forget that. He was not to blame. She must keep her tears to herself until she was alone. Never show either temper or distress; and if he wanted her to peacock about in all the jewellery in the world — well, she would, since he wanted it.

So she schooled herself to tranquillity and Christopher had no idea of the stony path by which she had reached it.

To her surprise, there was something almost like eagerness in Christopher's voice when he greeted her.

"Karen, I'm sorry I upset you last night. I — I had the devil in me yesterday! And, anyhow, you were quite right! Most of that stuff is in appalling taste! No wonder you jibed! I salute your superior instinct!"

"Oh, but they are lovely!" Karen protested. "It's I that am wrong! I'm not the right sort of person to show them off properly and I felt — silly and self-conscious."

He looked at her thoughtfully.

"Yes; that's quite true. They don't suit you. But——" — he fumbled under his pillow — "there is something I do wish you'd wear. Damn the thing! I can't reach it!"

"Let me help," Karen said eagerly and bent over him. Somehow or other, the box he wanted to get out had got caught in the opening of the pillow case and Karen had to bend so low that she could feel the warmth of his breath fanning her cheek. And, suddenly, she became intensely aware of his nearness.

Then, with heightened colour, she stood erect and laid the case in his hand.

He contrived to open it and lifted out the pearls.

"Will you wear these?" he asked, holding them out to her, and then, as she hesitated, he added: "Believe me, they will suit you. In fact, they are somehow like you."

She looked at the lovely, almost luminous string and the tears started to her eyes. No woman could possibly be insensible to such a compliment, and as she took them from his hand she bent swiftly and impulsively brushed his cheek with her soft, unpainted lips.

"I'll be proud to," she whispered.

She put them on in front of the mirror and turned for his approbation but — something had happened. The friendliness had vanished and a curtain of impersonality had descended.

"Now tell me about Madame Zelia," he ordered as she came and sat down in the chair beside his bed.

Karen suppressed a sigh. Just for a moment or two she had felt near to Christopher. Now she was shut out again.

She found that she had to act as Christopher's secretary.

"Usually my cousin, Fred Thirlby, helps me run the place," he explained. "And he will be coming back in a few weeks to take over even more. At present he is — on his honeymoon."

"I see," she said quietly, wondering what this cousin would think of her advent. "Have you — have you told him about — us?"

"Not yet," he hesitated. "As a matter of fact, I want you to see about that. Have it put in the paper. I'm afraid that will mean we get newspaper reporters down here, but we need not see them. We'll rough out some sort of story for them and you can type it out. Can you type, by the way?"

"A little," she admitted cautiously.

He did not appear to be listening, and since he was obviously thinking something out, she sat in silence.

"The day before it goes in the paper, I want you to pay a visit to my old aunt a few miles farther on to the sea. Apart from Fred, she is my only relative, and I prefer that she should be told of our marriage before it is made public property. Her name is Sarah Thirlby and, actually, she's a great-aunt. I shall be glad if you will show her every courtesy, even though she is unlikely to show you any!"

"Oh!" Karen said blankly. "She sounds — frightening!"

"She is," Christopher said feelingly. "Twenty years ago she gave me a tanning that I can remember to this day.

60

All because I'd scrounged a few apples. How was I to know that she was keeping those specially to give me on my birthday?"

Karen laughed and, in spite of the awe-inspiring portrait that he painted of the old lady, decided that she would — must — make a friend of her. For here was someone who could tell her all about Christopher. But not in a hurry.

She drew a mental picture of Miss Thirlby — tall, still handsome, white hair, immaculate in a rather old-fashioned black silk gown with white lace at her throat and wrists — possibly a stick to support her — a commanding personality who was used to giving orders and having them obeyed. As Christopher was.

She realised that he was speaking.

"I had Bannister bring the record player in here," he was saying. "Did you get that record?"

"Yes; and some others," she said eagerly. "I hope you don't mind. But I asked them if there were any more like that and they found one for me. And on the other side there was a lovely tune as well. Children singing. So I got that. And they were playing something in the shop and that was nice, so I — so I——"

"You've been really dashing it," he commented, evidently amused.

"Oh, that wasn't the worst of it," she confessed shyly. "I — I hope you don't mind, Christopher, but I bought you a wedding present!"

"Did you indeed!" he sounded amused, she thought, but not unkindly so.

"Yes," she rushed on. "It's this," and she held out a small black box.

"Unpack it for me," he said quietly and her heart ached at the realisation that even a simple thing like unpacking a gift was beyond him now.

"It is unpacked," she assured him. "It's a baby wireless, Christopher. Look, you just touch this spring——" The lid flew open and immediately music began to pour out.

"Well I'm damned!" he exclaimed. "Here, let's have a look!"

She had not seen him as eager as this over anything yet and she showed off the tiny box of tricks happily.

61

"Look. You see, you can alter the station with one finger and the same with the volume. They showed me. I thought it could lie on your bed and you could — could do it all yourself, Christopher."

There was an unconscious note of pleading in her voice, as if she were begging him to like her gift to him, but Christopher did not speak. His lips were pressed together and his face had that shut look.

She gave a little gulp. She had meant to give him pleasure and all she had done was to remind him of his helplessness. Suddenly she jumped to her feet and ran out of the room. He must not see her cry.

But later, passing his room door, she heard the little wireless playing and a smile returned to her face. Perhaps, after all, she had not made yet another mistake.

She decided that she would walk to Miss Thirlby's house, partly because it was a lovely day for October and partly because she did not want to give the impression that she was showing off the fact that she now had the command of all Christopher's wealth.

Rather to her surprise, Miss Thirlby's house turned out to be a cottage. A very lovely one with a thatched roof and oak timbered walls, but still a cottage. The garden, however, was what really caught one's eye. It was a mass of colour that put even Christopher's to shame, larger though it was. And in the garden was a short, stocky woman in well-worn tweeds grubbing about in the earth with ungloved hands. A companion, probably, Karen thought. But when she asked timidly if Miss Thirlby was in, the woman got up and looked at her curiously.

"I am Miss Thirlby," she said curtly. "Who are you? I don't buy things at the door."

"I don't sell them," Karen said with a little flush of annoyance. "Christopher asked me to come and see you. I — am his wife," she finished awkwardly.

Miss Thirlby looked her up and down with frank curiosity.

"Well I'm damned!" she said frankly. "So those stories are true, after all. I put them down to village gossip. But evidently the grape-vine system is more accurate than I realised! Well——" She hesitated. "Better tell me all about it out here, because if we go into the house, my maid — she's a village girl — will be listening at the door for certain. And we don't want that!"

She led the way to a small summer-house and indicated a seat.

"Cigarette?" she offered, fumbling in a capacious pocket. "No? Wish I didn't. But it's a habit now and I'm too old to worry about breaking it. Well, now tell me all about it!"

For a moment Karen hesitated, regretting that the picture of the elegant old lady that she had drawn had no substance in fact. This keen, shrewd-eyed woman was a disconcerting audience. It would be quite impossible to hide anything from her.

"There is not very much to tell," she said quietly. "Christopher asked me to marry him and I agreed. It was a very quiet affair."

"Naturally," Miss Thirlby nodded. And then, outrageously: "And just why did you agree?"

Karen pressed her soft lips together, rebellion in her heart. What right had this impossible person to ask her questions like that, even if she was Christopher's great-aunt? She would not answer them — she would not!

"Was it — his money?" Miss Thirlby asked softly, her bright eyes intent on Karen's downcast face.

"No; it was not," she said indignantly.

"No?" Miss Thirlby said indifferently. "Oh well, that's the rumour in the village. And, after all, it is understandable enough. Perhaps you would like to hear the whole story as I got it. They say that you and Christopher have only known each other since his accident and that no young girl ties herself up to a hopeless invalid on such a short acquaintance unless she's getting something out of it. I see you are wearing Monica's pearls," she finished unexpectedly.

Karen's hand flew to the pearls that Christopher had asked her to wear. Evidently this horrible woman thought that she had not wasted much time in making the most of her new position, and it was quite hopeless to tell her that, if Christopher had had his way, she would have been wearing very much more jewellery than that.

"Your story is quite true," she said quietly. "I met Christopher for the first time three days before we were married. And I was practically penniless. All the same, I did not marry him for his money."

Miss Thirlby frowned. On the face of it, that statement sounded incredible, and yet, against her better judgment, she found herself believing it.

"Well, if it wasn't that, what the deuce was it?" she asked bluntly, and yet with more kindness than she had yet shown to Karen.

Karen shook her head stubbornly, and after a minute Miss Thirlby began to speak almost as if she were talking to herself.

"If I were in Christopher's shoes, I know what I'd want to do," she mused. "And that is, crawl into my hole and hide myself. That's why I can't understand him giving a girl he knows nothing about the right to come into his room and stare at him."

"I don't!" Karen said indignantly. "Nobody could be so brutal as to do that! Oh — can't you understand?"

"Pity?" Miss Thirlby probed relentlessly. "You're a little fool if you let that run away with you. These fools of doctors say that he'll be dead in six months. How do they know? By rights, I ought to have died twenty years ago — according to the doctors. But I haven't. And I don't mean to for many a year yet. Well, was it pity?"

Had it been pity? To some degree, it must have been, Karen thought. But not an ordinary sort of pity. She had been sorry for Miss Cotton. But that emotion had had absolutely nothing in common with what she felt for Christopher. That was something that occupied her thoughts every moment of her waking day, that controlled every action, every decision she made. Something bigger than she was herself — something that was at once a joy and an agony.

"You'd better tell me," Miss Thirlby said quietly. "I know that I'm a rude old woman, but — I'm likely to be your best friend, none the less. Now then, what was it?"

Karen said nothing and then, abruptly, Miss Thirlby put her earth-stained hand under her chin and jerked it relentlessly up. She saw the soft, trembling lips, the quick colour that came and went and the pleading, pain-laden eyes. And her own rugged face expressed sheer consternation.

"My dear, not that!" she almost begged.

Karen nodded wordlessly and Miss Thirlby sighed deeply.

"My dear, why did you have to do that?" she asked in a troubled way. "Don't you realise——?"

"I — realise everything," Karen said steadily. "But — it doesn't make any difference. Nothing does when — when you love someone."

Miss Thirlby nodded.

"If you had said, 'when you are in love,' there might have been some hope for you," she commented. "But to love — that is a very different thing." She smiled grimly as she saw Karen's surprise at her understanding. "Yes; even I know that. Some sixty years ago—— But one doesn't forget. That's a woman's curse. Now then, what are you going to do about it?"

"Nothing — except to see that it doesn't annoy Christopher," Karen told her.

"Oh, you'll annoy him," Miss Thirlby told her frankly. "There's no human being that hasn't annoyed him at one time or another. You see, he has no patience with anybody who doesn't do exactly what he thinks they ought to. Never had. And I doubt if he's improved?" She cocked an enquiring eye at Karen, who smiled and shook her head.

"I didn't know him before his accident," she pointed out. "But——"

"But his illness hasn't made an angel of him," Miss Thirlby supplemented. "It never does — except in books and obituary notices. And Christopher has inherited a lot of his mother's temperament. A selfish little wretch if ever there was one. Expected the rest of the world to stand on its head if it suited her that it should."

"I wondered — Christopher said that his mother and father didn't — weren't——" Karen said hesitatingly.

"Didn't hit it off?" Miss Thirlby nodded. "They certainly did not. To begin with, Gerald, Christopher's father, was one of those appallingly possessive men. Expected his wife to have no existence apart from him. Monica, on the other hand, had been used to crowds of men around her ever since she was a child. So there was always trouble. Christopher grew up in an atmosphere of conflict and quarrels. And, of course, both of them were so immersed in their own affairs that they had absolutely no time or love to spare for him. As a matter of fact," she added thoughtfully, "I don't know that Christopher has ever had love from anybody in all his life."

"From you," Karen suggested softly.

Miss Thirlby shrugged her shoulders.

"Oh that!" she said disparagingly. "But what use was it to him? A great-aunt isn't much good to a boy. Too big an age-gap. Yes, Marigold, what is it?" she finished impatiently as a girl came towards them.

"Please, miss, it's the Vicar's wife on the telephone," the girl said, her eyes on Karen. "Says it's important."

"Oh dear! I shall have to answer it — and that means half an hour," Miss Thirlby told Karen. "Will you wait——?"

"I'm afraid I can't," Karen said regretfully. "But may I come again?"

"Do," Miss Thirlby said cordially. "For one thing, it may stop some of the gossip and, for another, I like you!"

"I like you," Karen returned smilingly. She turned to go and then remembered something. "Miss Thirlby, you asked me why I married Christopher. But you didn't ask why he married me!"

"No," Christopher's aunt said slowly. "I didn't have to ask that. You see, I guessed."

And without giving Karen a chance to ask her what she meant, she gave a curt nod and vanished into the cottage.

Karen had meant to pay her another visit within a day or two, but she was far too busy. She had to pay another visit to town for fittings at Madame Zelia's, and also it fell to her to issue the invitations for the house party that Christopher was determined to give.

"And soon," he said emphatically. "Fred and — his wife are coming back, and I want this to be a welcome to them!"

So she prepared lists, wrote, at Christopher's dictation,

to his proposed guests and held the sheets so that he could sign each one personally. She saw the beads of sweat on his forehead when he had finished and her heart sank when she thought of the strain that this house party was bound to cause.

"Give Mrs. Paynton the duplicate list," he said faintly when he had done. "Tell her to jot down what she thinks are suitable bedrooms and then bring the list back to me. Of course, she won't be able to do that until we get replies. Some of them won't be able to come, of course."

But, strangely enough, each reply was an acceptance, and when Karen passed on the information to Mrs. Paynton, the housekeeper clicked her tongue worriedly.

"That's awkward, madam," she told Karen, shaking her head. "You see, I didn't think to tell you at the time, because I thought naturally there would be some refusals. I suppose they don't hardly like to say 'No' in the circumstances, but we are going to be a bedroom short! Mr. Christopher must have forgotten that you are using one of the rooms, you see."

"Yes. But his present bedroom was previously a sitting-room," Karen pointed out. "There is still his old bedroom."

Mrs. Paynton pursed her lips.

"Yes, that's true, madam. But, you see — the fact is, we haven't liked to say anything to Mr. Christopher but — his room is just exactly as it was before his accident, poor gentleman. I was wondering whether it would be best just to say nothing to him and use it — or you move into it, madam?"

Karen hesitated. She shrank from the task of consulting Christopher and yet she hated the idea of doing anything behind his back. Finally she said:

"I think the only thing to do is just to say that it will be necessary to use his room — take it for granted that he realised that himself."

"Perhaps you are right, madam," Mrs. Paynton said a little doubtfully.

Considerably to Karen's relief, Christopher interrupted her before she got to the end of her explanation.

"Oh yes, I'd realised that," he said indifferently. "Put Fred and Stella in there, will you? And turn all my junk out — there's quite a lot of it. Burn it if you like."

"I'll see to it," Karen promised evasively and knew that every tiny thing that had belonged to Christopher when he was well would be cherished by her all her life.

It was rather heart-breaking to go into the room that had so obviously belonged to an athletic man who extracted the last ounce from life. There were wardrobes that held riding kit, every sort of sports outfit and evening clothes as well as more ordinary day-suits. There were tennis rackets, hockey sticks, boxing gloves. Karen breathed a little quivering sigh for the man who lay helpless downstairs. Was it any wonder that he was irritable and bitter?

Slowly she packed everything away, realising as she did so that Christopher must be a considerably taller man than she had realised. And then, suddenly, she stopped. Slowly she walked over to a little desk and looked from it to the bunch of keys that Christopher had given to her. This desk, too, must be cleared and yet she was sure that here must be held the personal and private part of Christopher's life. Letters. For the first time she wondered if there had ever been another woman than herself in Christopher's life. It seemed unlikely that such a good-looking, virile man as he had been could have got to the age of twenty-seven without having attracted some woman or other. And so she was half-diffident, half-afraid of opening the desk. She left it to last of all. And the minute she had opened it, she knew that she had been right. On the flat of the desk lay a leather photograph wallet. She picked it up and slowly opened it. On one side was a picture of Christopher himself, trim in riding breeches and an open-neck shirt, standing beside a horse. On the other side, the picture of a girl. Dark, strikingly good-looking. And scrawled across it, the words, "With all my love, darling."

For a moment Karen gazed at it. Then, with a little sob, she put it into one of the open trunks and resolutely got on with her job.

After all, what was there that she could do about it? And what did it matter? This girl was not Christopher's wife. She was. But in six months' time — only you didn't have to think of that. You had to take one day at a time.

Fred and his wife were to come before the other guests.

"To some extent, he'll have to be host," Christopher said grimly. "I want him to be here to help you."

Karen nodded and inwardly said a little prayer that Fred and his wife might be understanding and sympathetic. And that they would not ask too many questions.

On the day on which they were to arrive, she personally inspected their room to make sure that everything was quite perfect. Then she went slowly downstairs to await their arrival. Shortly before lunch-time, she heard the sound of a car and glanced a little anxiously out of the window.

A small, rakish sports car stood outside. Its occupants were a rather heavily built man who was already unstrapping luggage and a tall girl who was negligently standing by watching without offering any assistance.

A dark, handsome girl — the girl of the portrait she had found in Christopher's desk, who was also, it appeared, Fred's wife.

CHAPTER FIVE

FOR a moment Karen stood looking out of the window, a prey to half a dozen conflicting emotions.

Then swiftly she made her way through the hall, glancing at her reflection in one of the mirrors as she did so. Not for the first time she experienced deep gratitude towards Madame Zelia. For she had kept her word, and every one of the beautiful garments of which Karen was now the possessor was a triumph of skill and understanding. The peacock blue tweeds that she was wearing now with a cosy amber jumper were the brightest colours she had ever worn, but they were right and, what was more, right for her. They called a colour to her cheeks and a lustre to her eyes of which even Karen was aware. A softer shade of the same bluish green had been used for all her underclothes and two *négligées* that she had simply not dared to wear yet, so fragile were they. There was a crimson woollen housecoat that combined cosiness with a positively inspired cut that was frankly beyond Karen's comprehension, although she knew that she felt marvellously at ease in it. For evening dresses, Madame Zelia had turned to Victorian styles, though she had been careful not to exaggerate them. The result was not only delightful, but would be, Karen realised, quite a good setting for her to wear some of Christopher's mother's jewellery, so long as they were careful in their choice.

Christopher was propped up on an extra pillow, which brought back the abiding anxiety for him to Karen's heart. He became so easily tired. How on earth would he manage to get through the coming week without collapsing? And if he did collapse, he would hate it so because he would feel humiliated.

"If I were a different sort of person — cleverer," Karen thought regretfully, "I should know how to handle the situation so that he has all the rest he needs without feeling shut out from things. Oh well, I'll have to try!"

Christopher was a little flushed and she thought that he was breathing rather heavily, but his greeting sounded so

70

light-hearted that, against her better judgment, she was re-assured.

"Your cousin and his wife have come," she said and he put out his hand and caught hers.

"Have they?" he said, gently pulling her hand so that she had no choice but to sit on the edge of the bed. "We must give them a proper welcome, mustn't we, darling?"

Involuntarily, she started. It was the first time that Christopher had used an endearing term to her, and though she realised that it was quite a common thing for people to use them in ordinary conversation these days, it brought the colour to her cheeks. But she was not prepared for Christopher's soft laugh of triumph.

"So you're not just a complete little nun!" he teased her softly. "Or is it just that I have shocked you?"

"No — no, of course not," she stammered uncertainly.

"That's good," he said calmly. "Because if a man can't call his wife pretty names and pay her compliments, to whom can he pay them?"

Karen's soft lips quivered. That Christopher who had hardly seemed aware of her as an individual should be talking to her like this! It was incredible and completely beyond her comprehension, but her starved heart responded to it and all her love showed in her eyes. But Christopher's head was turned towards the door.

"Here they come!" he said, a note of excitement in his voice. "No; sit still. After all, you are my wife, you know!"

So, when Bannister opened the door and announced Fred and his wife, Stella, Karen was still a prisoner, held by Christopher's light clasp, so that the newcomers were treated to what must have appeared a very happy little domestic scene.

Ever so slightly, Stella Thirlby's eyes narrowed as she came through the door, but she lost none of her easy poise as she bent over Christopher and kissed him with casual warmth.

"Kit, my dear, you look splendid!" she said easily. "Doesn't he, Fred?"

Fred, advancing more slowly than his wife, held out his hand.

"It's good to see you again, old man!" he said simply,

and in the look which he and Christopher exchanged, Karen saw both affection and a deep friendship, and her own liking for Fred Thirlby started from that moment.

"Stella, Fred, I'm glad you've come!" Christopher said eagerly. "I wanted you to meet Karen before the rest of the crowd get here! Karen, these are the two best pals I've got! They'll be yours as well!"

"But of course," Stella said softly and, just as her liking for Fred had been born in a second, so did Karen's dislike and mistrust for this lovely girl begin. None the less, she played her part courageously.

Smilingly, she responded to their greetings, and if her heart was thumping at this, the first social gesture that she had ever made, they at least did not know it. And she had her reward for the effort she made, in seeing that Christopher was pleased.

He pulled her down beside him again and said, a little excitedly:

"We must have a drink to celebrate this! Karen——"

"I told Bannister to bring some immediately," Karen said tranquilly, thankful that she had remembered Mrs. Paynton's comment when she had first arrived at Claverings that it was the custom of the house to welcome guests with refreshments. "And some sandwiches."

"My dear, sandwiches at this time in the morning!" Stella laughed. "But we only had breakfast an hour or so ago! I couldn't eat a thing!"

"Well, I could!" Fred grumbled. "They called it breakfast, but it wasn't what I mean by breakfast! It never is in hotels. So I'll be glad."

Karen smiled at him, unconscious of the revealing gratitude in her eyes, and Fred Thirlby felt the shadow of uneasiness that had troubled him ever since he had heard of his cousin's marriage press more heavily. Just what sort of girl he had imagined it would be who would marry poor old Kit now that he was in this mess he did not quite know, but certainly not a sweet unsophisticated child like this! Perhaps Kit realised that. Perhaps that was why he had asked them to come first so that they could give her a bit more confidence, poor kid. Well, so far as he was able, she should have all the help she needed, and Stella, bless her, knew the ropes; she'd see that this show Kit was putting on went with a snap from the word "go."

"Who are coming down?" he asked Christopher over their drinks. "The usual gang?"

"Yes, the Cardews, Phil Lakin, the Denbys — yes, just the old lot," Christopher said, and to Karen's sensitive ears there was already a weary note in his voice. "Karen will show you the list — and where they are parked."

"Which room have you given us?" Stella asked casually from the window-seat. "Not that ghastly blue one, I do hope."

"No. I think Karen has put you in my old room. Haven't you, darling?" Christopher said, taking her hand in his again. "I expect Stella would like to go up——"

"Oh, yes, of course," Karen said hurriedly, standing up.

"Oh, plenty of time!" Stella said lightly, in a way that somehow made Karen feel as if she had tried to hustle her guest away. "Can I have another, Kit? You always have run a marvellous line in drinks!"

"Help yourself!" he said invitingly. "Liberty Hall, you know. It would be odd if — Fred's wife was not completely at home here!"

There was a little silence, during which Karen was acutely conscious of something in the air that was not the sort of hatred with which she had grown so familiar at Miss Cotton's, but — something worse just because it was so intangible. She shivered and, at the same instant there was a sharp little splintering sound, and with a little cry Stella stood up.

"Oh, how careless of me!" she exclaimed ruefully. "Kit, I've snapped the stem of my glass! How quite too unforgivable! And particularly after your pretty speech. I do hope that it was not one of a set!"

It was, as Karen knew quite well, but Christopher was smiling, and she took her cue from him.

"That doesn't matter in the least!" she said, taking the two pieces of glass from Stella. "But I do hope you haven't cut yourself — or spilled anything on your suit?"

"No," Stella drawled. "Fortunately, I haven't. Aren't you pleased, Kit?"

"Delighted," he said, still smiling. "Won't you have

another drink — it might help to settle your nerves."

"Darling, I haven't got such things!" she protested laughingly. "No; nothing more. I think I'll go upstairs. I know the way, Karen — isn't it? But do come with me. You and I must get to know one another!"

Silently, Karen followed her, feeling that in some odd way their positions had been reversed and that it was Stella who was the hostess and she who was the guest.

Neither girl spoke until they stood in Christopher's lovely old room; then, as she threw her trim little hat and driving gloves on to the bed, Stella said suddenly:

"Whose charming idea was it that we should have this room? Yours or Kit's?"

"Christopher's," Karen admitted. "I — I think he wanted you and your husband to have the pleasantest room there was, and it certainly is that."

"Oh, quite," Stella agreed drily. "It is the room that the current owner of Claverings has always used for himself — for generations. This is probably the first time that a guest has had it. It is, as I said, a charming idea!"

Karen did not reply. There was an undercurrent here that she did not understand, and she suddenly felt tired.

"Do ring if there is anything that you want, won't you?" she said mechanically, and went downstairs with the uncomfortable feeling that she had made an enemy — and lost the first round to her, though she did not quite understand how it had come about.

Stella, Karen learned, had always lived in the neighbourhood of Claverings, and as soon as lunch was over she announced her intention of looking up old friends.

"Unless, of course, you would prefer me to lend a hand over anything?" she asked Karen, as if she found the idea faintly amusing.

"Oh dear. She doesn't like me any more than I like her!" Karen thought regretfully. "And Christopher is so fond of them both!" But aloud she said: "No, I think everything is all right. Mrs. Paynton is amazingly efficient."

"H'm." Stella stubbed out her cigarette thoughtfully. "Well, if you will take my advice, you won't leave too much to her. I've always told Kit that. Not that it matters so much when it is a bachelor establishment, but a wife should be the mistress in her husband's home, you know."

Karen flushed at the implied criticism. She did leave a lot to Mrs. Paynton, she knew; but then, how could it be otherwise? After all, that was why she was there. Besides——

"I do leave a lot to her," Karen admitted. "But I think we are very lucky, because it leaves me more time to be with Christopher."

Stella pushed back her chair with an impatient gesture.

"Oh well, it's for you to decide!" she shrugged. "Are you coming to see the Robsons, Fred?"

"No; I don't think so," he said slowly. "Kit wants me to go through some papers with him and he wants me to give the stables the once-over as well. Briggs is a good man, but he works better under supervision."

Anyhow that, Karen thought with a sigh of relief, was something for which she could hardly be held responsible!

Stella went off in the little sports car, and Fred, who had seen her off, came slowly back into the room. He was the first to admit that he was neither a subtle nor a brainy chap. He seemed to think that it was a disadvantage, but if so, it was one that never troubled his friends, because even the most worldly of them was able to sense the loyalty and genuine kindness that were his principal characteristics. He smiled now, in a friendly and oddly reassuring way, to Karen as he sat down beside her.

"You and I must have a talk, Mrs. Kit," he said gently. "After all, I'm Kit's nearest relation and, I think, his best friend. So, you see, his choice of wife means a lot to me." His whole manner precluded any possible resentment on her part and she smiled her agreement.

"Tell me about the poor old chap first," he said quietly. "Do you think it is true that there is no chance of his recovery?"

"That is what all but one of the specialists say," Karen admitted sadly. "And that one said only a miracle could cure him."

"Poor old chap!" Fred said feelingly. "And there isn't any improvement? I saw he had the use of one hand."

"He had right from the beginning," Karen explained. "I think he is getting a little more adroit at using it, but it does not seem to me to be getting very much stronger."

Fred nodded. It had been a terrible shock to him to see the man whom he had always loved and admired lying a complete wreck before him.

"You must have thought it odd that I didn't come back when it happened," he commented heavily. "But the fact is, we didn't hear about it for quite a while and then Stella wasn't fit to travel — funny thing, but actually we got married on the very day that it happened. As a matter of fact, it must have been within an hour or so of the crash, although we did not know at the time. Stella met me at Euston — I'd been in Scotland fishing — and asked me if I still felt the same about things. I've been pestering the poor girl for years, you know. Naturally, it shook me rather, because I'd practically given up hope. Not quite, though. That's how it happened that I had the licence all ready. You never quite know with Stella what she'll do next, so I thought I'd better be prepared. As a matter of fact, I'd always thought she was keen on" — he stopped and cleared his throat — "on someone else. But it turned out that I was the lucky chap!" He beamed at Karen, and she, encouraged by his rather naïve revelations, found the courage to say shyly:

"I expect *our* marriage was rather a surprise, wasn't it?"

"Well, yes, frankly it was," he admitted rather awkwardly. With a clumsy, kindly gesture, he took one of Karen's hands in his big one. "You've got some pluck, little Mrs. Kit. It isn't every girl that would take on what you have."

"Somebody had to look after him," she said simply. Then, without warning, her face crumpled up like an unhappy child's. "I *can't* believe he'll never walk again!" she sobbed. "Or that he's going to — going to——"

"No; nor can I," Fred agreed. "When I came into his room, I thought to myself that he looked as if he'd come in tired after a day's hunting and was just having a rest before getting on with the next thing. That's what made me ask you if there wasn't any chance."

They sat in silence for a few minutes, and then Karen dried her tears and said hesitatingly:

"About this house party——"

"Yes, I was going to ask you about that. Surely it's damn' silly with him in this mess?"

"I suppose so — if there is any chance of him getting better. But he doesn't think that there is, you see. So he is determined to live the rest of his life as nearly as he can to normal. Of course, it's only a travesty of the real thing, but — he so hates pity and the realisation that he is helpless. So — it is in the nature of a gesture — a defiance of Fate, really. That's why I couldn't try to dissuade him."

"No," Fred agreed slowly. To himself he was saying: "Well, I'm damned. The kid is really fond of him! That yarn Stella got hold of about her marrying him for his money must be all my eye! More likely they've known each other for a long time and we didn't know about it. After all, a chap's relations don't always know everything about him! Think I'll go and see Aunt Sarah to-morrow and see what she makes of it all! Never knew a woman that could take her in!"

He realised that Karen was saying quietly:

"I am very much afraid that it may make him worse, but — Christopher is not the sort of person you can give advice to. He will have to find out for himself. Only — if there is anything that you can do to keep him from getting too tired, I'll be awfully glad!"

"I will, my dear. I will," Fred promised, considerably troubled at the situation she had outlined. "So will Stella, I'm sure. She and Kit have always been great pals."

"Yes." Try as she would, Karen could not keep the chilly note out of her voice. Fred, she could tell, adored his lovely wife, and suddenly, quite absurdly, Karen felt herself concerned for him. He was the sort of person that one would hate to get hurt, she thought. He would be so terribly vulnerable. And then and there she made up her mind that, no matter how difficult it was, she would be just as nice to Stella as if she really liked her. Though it would not be easy.

The remaining guests arrived at intervals during the next day and Karen spent most of the time with Christopher, since he wanted them both to receive their visitors.

He was in high spirits and it was obvious that more than

one newcomer felt relieved when they had once met him. It was easy to suppose, Karen thought, that they had been torn between a desire to fall in with Christopher's wishes from sheer sympathy and a reluctance to see him in his present condition. Friendship had evidently triumphed. And, possibly, she imagined, a certain amount of curiosity about herself had helped.

For they *were* curious. She was conscious that little knots of people would be chattering as she approached them and would then lapse into silence. It would have been rather hurtful if they had not been such obviously good-hearted people.

She did her best to join in with the chatter and fun that was going on, but half the jokes passed over her head and she had no knowledge of many of the things about which they were all talking. She might perhaps have asked Christopher to give her a few pointers, but he was rarely alone and the only two other people who might have helped her were Fred and Stella. Fred was quite fully occupied playing deputy host to Christopher, and Stella——

Karen's head went up proudly. She knew now that she had not been mistaken in thinking that Stella disliked her. Almost immediately the others had arrived, she began, subtly but unmistakably, to put Karen in the shade.

It was she who, time after time, led the conversation on to topics which meant that Karen was left out. She also had a name, apparently, for mixing drinks, and there was always a little cluster of men round her laughing and joking as she made up "specials" to suit each one of them.

Actually it always was the men who were attracted to Stella. Women seemed to avoid her, but that Karen did not notice. She only realised that she must have disappointed Christopher. More than once she had seen his eyes on her with an expression which she could read, only too clearly, as either irritation or chagrin. She, his wife, was letting him down in front of his friends. An unforgivable sin and yet — how could it be otherwise?

"Why did he choose me and not one of them?" she thought wearily. "Sometimes I could wish that I had never——"

But that was not true, and she knew it. On any terms,

it was better to be with Christopher than to have gone through life not knowing of his existence.

"And there are things that I can do for him," she thought desperately. "At least, I could — before these people came! Perhaps when they go——"

But in the meantime, they were very much there and she was helpless.

"If I were different——" she thought miserably. "But one can only be oneself——"

She was terribly worried, too, about Christopher. In confidence, she had asked Bannister how Christopher was sleeping and it was a far from reassuring report that she heard.

"Dreadful, madam!" the man told her, shaking his head. "All last night, I could hear him." Bannister slept in Christopher's day-room, so that he was within easy call. "Not that he can move much, poor gentleman, but — I could tell. And this morning, he looked like a ghost. If this goes on much longer, he's going to collapse. He's in pain, too. I had to give him an extra injection yesterday, and if that keeps on, he won't get any good out of them."

"Oh, Bannister!" Karen looked at him in consternation. "What can we do?"

The man shook his head.

"I did suggest having Dr. Stalham along," he said. "But Mr. Christopher got furious. Said he wasn't going to have any more quacks making money out of him. Sometimes I think they didn't ought to have told him he wouldn't get better. It makes him reckless."

"I know," Karen nodded. "But I expect he made them tell him. I wonder — if the doctor had to come to the house for something else — suppose I weren't well, or something. Then he could see Christopher — just to reassure him about me."

Bannister shook his head.

"He'd see through that," he said and Karen had to admit that it was true.

"I'll try to think of something," she promised.

She went to Christopher and found him, for a wonder, alone. He held a glass in his hand, though, and Karen realised that it was far from being the first drink that he had had. That was not like him and made her anxious, too.

He glanced up as she came in and saluted her with the little glass.

"Hallo, my sweet. Here's to you!" he said, draining it. Karen sat down beside him and took the empty glass.

"Where is everybody?" she asked in an attempt to sound perfectly natural.

"Out — riding my horses over my land!" he laughed harshly. "Rather a joke that, isn't it? They are out enjoying themselves — and I am lying here a completely useless log!"

She laid her warm hand over his cold one.

"Christopher — don't you think it was a mistake?" she began.

"A mistake?" he said sharply. "What?"

"Having all these people here," she said quietly. "I mean — doesn't it make it harder for you to bear."

He drew a long deep, shuddering sigh.

"In some ways," he admitted. "But — there are recompenses."

"Are there?" she said doubtfully. "You thought that getting more tired might make you sleep at night. But it doesn't, does it?"

He looked at her with eyes that were resentful and angry.

"Who told you that?" he demanded. "Bannister?"

"Only because I asked him," she said hurriedly. "He could hardly refuse to answer me, could he?"

"No; I suppose not," he admitted and fell silent, his eyes fixed on the peep of garden that he could get from his window.

For a moment Karen hesitated. Then she said timidly: "Christopher, I'm sorry."

His eyes came back slowly to hers. Haunted, troubled eyes that spoke of pain both mental and physical.

"Are you? What for?" he asked in a curiously gentle voice.

"I'm — afraid I'm rather a disappointment to you, aren't I?" she said regretfully.

"A disappointment?" he said sharply. "No; certainly not. What made you think that?"

She made a little gesture of self-deprecation.

"I'm not like your friends."

"No; you're not," he admitted gravely. "But doesn't it occur to you that I might, perhaps, have married one of them instead of you if I had felt that I wanted their constant companionship?"

She was foolishly pleased and smiled at him with misty eyes.

"Then you don't want me to be able to — mix drinks and — and gossip?" she asked, still a little anxious.

"God forbid!" he said fervently. He hesitated for a moment. Then, almost as if he were speaking against his will he went on: "As long as I can remember, I've liked people's company — up to a point. After that point comes, I've always wanted to be alone. That's why I used to fly — one of the reasons." He looked at her in a puzzled way, as if he could not quite understand why he was taking her into his confidence.

She gave his hand a gentle little squeeze.

"If ever I come here and you would prefer to be all alone, you'll tell me, won't you?" she said earnestly.

"Oh — you——" he said thoughtfully. "No — somehow or other, you don't trespass. You seem to merge into the background."

To most women it would have sounded rather a doubtful compliment, but to Karen's ears it was sheer music. Other people he wanted to get rid of. But not her.

She went to the little drawer where she kept her needlework and quietly sat down in the window seat with it.

"How is it getting on?" Christopher asked, and she held it up.

"Rather slowly," she admitted. And then, because the colouring of the peacock reminded her, she said suddenly: "Stella goes to Madame Zelia as well, doesn't she?"

"Yes; I believe she does," he said indifferently. "What made you think of that?"

"Oh — I don't know. There is something about her clothes that is similar — the same colours, only brighter."

She did not tell him that this very brightness had become singularly trying. It had the effect of making her feel blotted out by Stella's brilliance as well as by her manner.

"I suppose they do get into rather a rut," Christopher agreed casually. "You'd better try somewhere else next time."

She was about to reply when Fred came rather hurriedly into the room.

"I say, Karen, could you lend us a hand?" he said almost peremptorily for him. "Mrs. Cardew has taken a bit of a toss — nothing serious. Ankle and bruises as far as we can make out. But Mrs. Paynton isn't about and none of the other women seem to know what to do."

"Of course," Karen said quickly and followed him out of the room.

They had carried Mrs. Cardew up to her room and several women were standing rather helplessly around. They drew back as Karen came in and she went swiftly over to the bed.

Fortunately, Mrs. Cardew had been wearing jodhpurs and low boots and so it was possible to attend to the already swollen ankle more easily than if she had been wearing top-boots.

Karen examined it carefully.

"I think you ought to have the doctor," she said quietly. "But in the meantime, I can make it a little bit more comfortable for you."

And, by the time the doctor had arrived, she had got Mrs. Cardew into bed with a cold bandage round her ankle giving her all the relief that was possible.

Dr. Stalham examined it carefully and commented graciously that it was a nice piece of work.

"In fact, I'm only taking it off because I want to have a look at the ankle," he admitted. "H'm. Probably a straight-forward strain. In any case, we'll have to wait until the swelling is down before we take an X-ray. Now, how about a nurse, Mrs. Thirlby?"

He looked with some curiosity at the quiet girl who had shown such competence and Karen shook her head.

"If you think I can manage it and Mrs. Cardew doesn't mind, I'd like to nurse her," she suggested.

Dr. Stalham glanced at Mrs. Cardew.

"My dear, if it isn't an awful fag, I'd love it," she confessed. "I can't stand nurses — too starched and full of their own importance. But I shall probably be a complete pest! I'm not very patient, you know!"

"I'll take a chance," Karen said lightly, and Mrs. Cardew's bright eyes glinted with surprise and curiosity. She was, she realised, going to be in a very favourable position for finding out a bit about this girl.

On the way downstairs, Karen quickly made her request to the doctor, who nodded understandingly.

"Overdoing it, eh?" he said sympathetically. "Well, I'll probably be able to tell you at a glance, but I doubt if it will do much good. Thirlby isn't one to take orders, you know."

"I know," Karen admitted. "But — I must know. And, Dr. Stalham, I want to find out who it was that said Christopher had got a chance. I might — want to get in touch with him."

Dr. Stalham paused.

"My dear, you mustn't build on that," he said gently. "It's the outside chance — the miracle."

"I know," she admitted. "But then — I believe in miracles, you see. So — will you find out, please? I expect the nursing-home would tell you, wouldn't they?"

"Oh yes; they would do that," he sighed and shook his head. "Well — let's make our report, shall we?"

Christopher listened in silence, thanked him, but frowned when he heard of Karen's offer.

"She's got enough to do as it is," he insisted.

"No, really, I haven't," she insisted eagerly. "The staff knows just what to do without any orders and——" She stopped, on the point of saying that Stella had so usurped her position of hostess that she wouldn't be missed when she remembered the doctor's presence and amended it to: "I should like to look after Mrs. Cardew, Christopher. I can — I mean, I am competent to."

"You certainly are," Dr. Stalham said briskly. "Well, that's that! How are you feeling, Thirlby."

"Fine!" Christopher said casually.

"And that was a black lie," the doctor said to Karen when they had left him. "The man's as ill as he knows how to be. How he's putting up a show like that is beyond me. He must have a will like steel! Ah well, send for me any time you think I can be of help, and in the meantime, I'll certainly get that address for you, Mrs. Thirlby."

Karen went back to her new patient, found her drowsing comfortably under the influence of the mild sedative that the doctor had given to her, and set about tidying the room. She could not tell anybody so, but she was grateful for this new job.

"Were you a nurse?" Mrs. Cardew asked as she watched Karen's nimble fingers binding her ankle one day. Like them all, she had her full share of curiosity about her hostess.

"No," Karen answered carefully. "But I have done quite a lot of nursing. Relatives, I mean. That's all."

"Well, you've certainly got the gift. In fact, you're a lot more gentle than many of them I've known. But then, they always regard you as a case, not a human being."

"Perhaps they have to," Karen suggested. "One could not bear to have one's feelings continually harrowed, so perhaps they have to become hard."

"M'm." Mrs. Cardew realised that she had got absolutely nothing out of the girl, but none the less the interview left her thoughtful, and when one of the other women came up for a pre-dinner gossip, she was still in a contemplative frame of mind.

"How is the little hostess looking after you?" her visitor asked curiously.

"Marvellously," Mrs. Cardew said firmly. "I'm beginning to wonder if all the tales we've heard are true. She doesn't seem that sort to me."

"But, my dear, I don't blame her even if they are true," the other woman replied. "After all, she'd be a complete fool if she hadn't grabbed the chance of easy money!"

"Is it so easy?" Mrs. Cardew demanded. "Would you like to have taken it on? I know I wouldn't!"

"Oh, of course, I know. Christopher must be a handful! After all, he always was! He must be many times worse now! All the same, it's only for six months. And look at the reward!"

And Karen, who had gone downstairs to supervise the tray that was to come up to Mrs. Cardew, stood petrified outside the partially open door. To go in now would completely embarrass the two women who were chatting so confidentially. And besides that — she lacked the courage.

It did not surprise her to hear what they thought of her, but it hurt none the less. She could, of course, have tip-toed away again, but they might hear her.

"It's true then, about him leaving her all his money?" Mrs. Cardew asked eagerly.

Mrs. Denby laughed.

"My dear, can't you tell that from our dear Stella's manner?" she asked. "She's simply livid! She thought she was dodging all the bother and yet making sure of the money by marrying Fred! And now Christopher has married this girl and Fred loses his inheritance — it isn't entailed, you know. A nasty revenge, isn't it? Kit made a mistake, though, in choosing such a mouse. It's almost too easy for Stella with her — peculiar talents!"

"She isn't a mouse," Mrs. Cardew said almost indignantly. "She's got something."

"Has she?" In her mind's eye, Karen could see the shrug of the shoulders that accompanied the remark. "Well, I can't see it and, believe me, nor can Stella."

"Fred can," Mrs. Cardew said briefly.

"Oh — Fred! He'd see good in the Witch of Endor!"

"I think he would," Mrs. Cardew agreed. "After all, he can see it in Stella!"

There was a little rustle and Mrs. Denby said:

"Well, I must go and get changed."

Karen flew. There was nothing else for it. She must not be found here listening. She reached her room and sat down, breathless and with a mind that ached with the hurt of what she had heard. Not immediately could she piece together just what it all meant.

They had spoken of Christopher's revenge. But revenge for what? And then she remembered that photograph in Christopher's room on which Stella had scrawled: "With all my love!"

She had *meant* that — at least, in so far as Stella could mean that she loved anyone but herself. She and Christopher — they could not have been engaged because, if they had, Fred would have known. But there must have been some sort of understanding.

Yet how could that be since she had married Fred?

And then she remembered the confidence that Fred had given her. Stella had made up her mind very suddenly that she would marry him. Karen frowned in an effort to remember just what he had said. She had rung him up *after* Christopher's accident, although Fred had not then heard of it. But had Stella? Those women seemed to think so. What was it that she had said?

"She thought that she was dodging all the bother and yet making sure of the money by marrying Fred."

Yes, that fitted in. Karen shivered a little at the thought of a woman who, loved by two such men as Christopher and Fred, could so play one off against the other as she had evidently done, and then quite coolly make up her mind to leave Christopher to his broken life and marry the man who would one day have his money.

"Oh, but she couldn't have done a thing like that!" All Karen's nature revolted at the thought. "No woman could."

And then Stella and what she had done suddenly became of no importance whatever, for Karen remembered something else that Mrs. Denby had said:

"And now Christopher has married this girl and Fred loses his inheritance. A nasty revenge, isn't it?"

For a moment she could not grasp the full horror of what that meant. Then, as at last she realised the truth, she buried her face in her shaking hands as if to shut it out.

But there was no escape.

At last she knew why Christopher had married her.

CHAPTER SIX

STELLA was in a thoughtful and rather edgy frame of mind. Not, she thought irritably as she brushed her thick hair, that it was to be wondered at. The strain that she had undergone since Kit's crash would have been one too many for most women.

First of all, the terrible shock when Ben Stringer had rung her up and told her of the crash. Ben worked on the technical side of the firm for whom Kit had acted as test pilot, and he had thought that he was doing her a kindness in letting her know before it became that night's news in all the papers. She had thanked him mechanically because, even as she was hanging up the receiver, she was making her plans.

At any time in the last two years she could have married either Fred or Kit. Sometimes she wondered why she had ever hesitated because, though there were things to be said in Fred's favour, it was Kit who had the money. Besides, she was as near to loving him as it lay in her nature to do. As long as she could remember, it had irked her that she was a woman. If you can dominate, you would be a fool not to, was her creed. And in Kit she saw all the ruthlessness, all the independence, all the fearlessness that she wanted for herself.

Only slowly had it penetrated her consciousness that in her woman's beauty she had a potent weapon which the strongest of men found irresistible. She had power! And she would use it as ruthlessly as Kit used his. The first thing to do was to find out what she did want — and that was not easy.

For it was not only being a girl that had handicapped Stella. Lack of money had been another factor. As long as she remembered, the too-big house which her father would not sell had been shabby, and cheeseparing had been the order of the day. It had been a passionately held tenet of hers that, somehow or other, sooner or later, she would be *rich!* And, as her beauty developed, she realised that there was no need for her to struggle and strive to make her way in a man-ruled world. Some man should do it for her. Fred she could have married any day that she had lifted her little finger and, admittedly, he had position to offer her. But he was not so wealthy as Kit by a good long way. And, in any case, it seemed so tame to marry a man who asked nothing better of life than that you should marry him. Now Kit — that was different! Her blood had pulsed at the thought of compelling an arrogant man like him to kneel at her feet. Nor had he surrendered easily, but when he had, she had experienced such triumph as she had never known before. And the instinct to play her fish just a little longer had been irresistible.

That was the way that things were when Kit had crashed and everyone, with perhaps the exception of Fred, had known it perfectly well. In that moment of horror she had realised only too clearly what everyone would expect of her, that she would marry Kit. Her hard, ruthless little jaw had set resolutely. Never, if she could do anything to prevent it!

Methodically, she sized up the situation. Fred was in the train on the way down from Scotland. He was coming straight to see her. She glanced at the clock. He should be at Euston in half an hour — there was just time. She would meet him and before there was any chance for him to see a paper, they would get married. Fred, she knew, had taken out a licence for their marriage and they could be married then and there. They could catch a plane for Paris — no, somewhere small where news would not seep through too quickly — and though people would be surprised, they simply couldn't know about Ben having 'phoned her, particularly as Ben was going to Argentina or Chile within a day or so.

Only in the taxi on her way to Euston had she realised something else. If Kit died, Fred would have all his money. Her heart gave a little leap. This was not just escape from what would be almost a living death — Ben had said that if Kit lived, he would be a hopeless crock. Fred took on the aspect of something more than a mere haven. He became the man through whom she could achieve her heart's desire.

Fred, the idiot, had been dazed and incredulous — but only too delighted to fit in with her plans. They were married and left England without Fred knowing of his cousin's disaster. And when they did at last hear, Stella had not been well enough to travel. And there was no need for her to lie about that. For, so their informant wrote, Kit had only a few months to live. Stella experienced a sense of frustration that almost made her scream. If only she had acted with her usual deliberation instead of letting her fears run away with her! She should have married Kit — and made the best of it for the short time that he had to live. And then — she would have been independent for the rest of her life. For, undoubtedly, Kit would have left her everything and she need not have worried to marry poor, infatuated, boring Fred! Oh, it was infuriating!

Still, there were compensations. As things were, Fred would get the money and that would be the next best thing to having it herself.

And then had come the news of Kit's amazing marriage, and for the first time in her life Stella was really afraid. Kit must, of course, know about her marriage to Fred and he guessed her reasons for it. And this was his revenge. A pretty thorough one, she had to admit.

It was not until she and Fred had actually reached Claverings that she realised just how thorough a revenge Kit had planned.

That girl, sitting on the edge of his bed, holding his hand; a charming little scene — if one did not remember what a short time ago it was that Kit had held her, Stella, in his arms and sworn that there could never be any other woman for him. But that was not all. The girl's appearance; not only her clothes, which were obviously Zelia's creations and just too similar to her own choice of colours for it to be a coincidence. Her colouring, her build, were much the same as her own. There, of course, the likeness stopped. Karen was a nonentity. But nobody would ever have thought of calling Stella that. Still, even if there was no likeness at all, it would not have mattered. For what Kit meant her to understand was that this girl was to have everything that might so easily have been hers. That same mocking spirit showed in the fact that she and Fred had been put in Kit's own room — the room that would have been hers had she been mistress of Claverings. As it was, she was to have it long enough to realise the luxury of it and then — she was to be turned out. Oh yes, Kit had been very clever!

Of course, there was only one thing to do. One had just to accept the situation and deny Kit the pleasure of seeing that he had hit hard and shrewdly. As for the girl, she simply did not matter. And, in any case, it was so ridiculously easy to make her squirm that it hardly afforded Stella any satisfaction, though she did spare a passing thought to the rather amazing fact that such a girl could have been sufficiently tough to take on the job that Kit had asked of her. You would have expected sophistication, not mousiness. Of course — Stella shrugged her lovely shoulders — still waters run deep. One never quite knows.

Just to-day, there had been something different about the girl. There had been that odd look in her eyes when she had heard one of the servants call her, Stella, "My lady."

It had obviously surprised her and she had said slowly: "I didn't know you had a title."

Stella had shrugged her shoulders.

"Naturally. Fred is a baronet. Didn't you know?" she had said, half impatiently, half amused.

"No — I didn't." Karen was looking at her very curiously. "But, of course — it explains——" She had pressed her pale lips together as if she thought that she had said too much, but if it had not been absurd, Stella would have sworn that there was scorn in the grey eyes.

Oh well, suppose there was! What did it matter? What harm could Karen do to her that she had not already done? Stella picked up her pearls. Actually she had been told that she was one of the people that should not wear pearls because they discoloured on her. But she loved them. They were so smooth, so reassuring, so very lovely. But not, she thought with sudden irritation, nearly such a good string as those that Karen was wearing!

She gave a sudden, angry little tug at them and the fine silk broke and a few pearls rolled to the floor. She picked them up carefully, angry with herself for having lost her temper. Now she had nothing to wear that would go with

90

the flame-coloured dress that she was wearing and, on this night of all nights during the week, every woman would be wearing all the jewellery she could.

For to-morrow the party would break up, but this evening, after dinner, a whole lot more people from round about had been invited. There would be dancing and general hilarity and there would be a lot of curious eyes on Stella. She shrugged her shoulders and went downstairs without waiting for Fred.

Karen was standing by the big hall fire as she came down, and with intense annoyance Stella saw that she, too, was wearing a flame-coloured dress on which her pearls showed to exquisite advantage. Stella's eyes narrowed. She meant to have a word with Madame Zelia when she got back to Town. It was intolerable that this girl's clothes should so resemble hers — although with a subtle difference, of course. Stella knew perfectly well that her own clothes were challenging. By no stretch of the imagination could Karen's be called that. All the same——

Karen had been sitting on the leather-padded curb to the fire, but as Stella came down she got up. At a glance, she realised, as Stella had, that they were dressed far too much alike for their own comfort, and a little ghost of a sigh escaped her lips. This was just one more thing that brought home inescapably the reason why Christopher had married her. And just one more thing about which she could do absolutely nothing.

"Would you like a drink?" she asked gravely. "The men are not down yet, but——"

Stella nodded and poured herself out a good stiff drink. Then, with it in her hand, she sauntered over to Karen and regarded her thoughtfully.

"Zelia?" she asked casually.

Karen flushed and nodded.

"I think you and I will have to come to some sort of arrangement with that lady," Stella suggested. "She seems to imagine that because we have married into the same family we must necessarily be dressed in the same colours, with the result that we simply kill one another."

"Oh no," Karen said quickly. "At least, it does you no harm. You are a much more vivid personality than I am."

Stella stared at her incredulously. There had been neither admiration nor despair in the girl's voice. Just a mere statement of fact from which there was no appeal. It left Stella at something of a loss to find a reply and before she had thought of a suitable one, Karen went on: "In any case, I shall not be having any more clothes from Madam Zelia. Christopher suggested that I should go to someone else."

"Did he?" Stella said blankly. Now what in the world did that mean? Had Kit repented or did it simply mean that he had realised his little plot had misfired? She would have shrugged the whole thing away but that she suddenly realised the girl was looking at her in a curious analytical way. Her hand went up to her throat. "I've broken my pearls," she commented for something to say. "It's rather a nuisance, because I've nothing else with me that goes with the dress."

Karen was about to murmur condolences when suddenly Christopher's voice surprised both of them. He had been wheeled in on the mobile day bed by Bannister and the thickly cushioned tyres had made no sound.

"Broken your pearls?" he said sympathetically. "How annoying. Karen, can't you lend Stella something?"

She gave a little start.

"Oh yes, of course," she said hurriedly. "I'll fetch some of the boxes, shall I?"

"Oh don't worry!" Stella said airily. "I shouldn't feel comfortable wearing anything that didn't belong to me! Suppose I lost something!"

The same old game again! Kit evidently could not think up anything new!

But Christopher would not listen to her protests. He inspected her gravely with eyes that stripped every shred of self-respect from her.

"Not rubies," he murmured "Diamonds? No, on the whole, I think not. What about emeralds, Stella? I don't know very much about these things, but I imagine that they would 'go' with that colour?"

She knew perfectly well that the result would be barbaric and crude, but recklessly she caught up the gauntlet he had thrown down. She would wear them — and get away with it. She would *be* barbaric — and desirable.

"That would be lovely, Kit dear," she agreed softly.

Karen slipped away to the safe and the two that were left waited in a silence that neither of them had the inclination to break. When Karen came back she held out the cases to Stella, who took them eagerly. She had always known that Kit's mother had had some marvellous jewellery, but she had never seen any of it before. Involuntarily, she gave a little gasp as she opened the cases and revealed the lovely things. A heavy necklet whose square cut emeralds were framed in diamonds and two wide bracelets to match.

"Put them on," Kit ordered, his eyes intent on her face.

Without any further protest, Stella did as she was told. She had a little trouble with the catch of one of the bracelets and Karen said quietly:

"Let me!" After all, there was nothing else that she could do and fortunately, she thought, neither Stella nor Christopher would realise that she was careful not to touch Stella's flesh. That, somehow, would be intolerable.

Fred came down a little later and looked rather anxiously at Kit.

"I say, old man, are you sure you're not overdoing it?" he asked.

"Good Lord, no!" Christopher said, his dark brows knitting in a sudden scowl. "Don't be such an old woman, Fred! Take a look at your missus. Doesn't she look terrific?"

There was a little silence as Fred took in the details of his wife's appearance. Then he said quietly:

"Stella always looks wonderful to me," and Karen felt a lump come into her throat.

She had wondered just how much Fred comprehended of the situation, and had come to the conclusion that in all probability no one would ever know that. Fred's love for his beautiful wife would make such a disclosure a disloyalty not to be contemplated.

For a moment a small shadow seemed to pass over Christopher's face; then it was quickly dispelled as the rest of his guests began to assemble. Under cover of all the chatter, Karen sought Bannister out.

"Bannister, Mr. Thirlby is very excited this evening," she

said anxiously. "Is it just because of everybody coming or——?"

Bannister shook his head. Like everyone else, he had been both startled and shocked at the news of Christopher's marriage, but without stopping to analyse the cause for it he had come to admit a great respect for the quiet girl to whom his beloved master's well-being evidently meant so much.

"He *is* excited," he admitted. "But — he made me give him a double injection half an hour ago. I didn't like doing it, madam, but — you know what he is when he insists."

"Yes," Karen sighed. "Look, Bannister, can you telephone to the doctor and tell him what has happened. He may be going out and I should like to know where we could get in contact with him."

"A very good idea, if I may say so, madam," Bannister agreed. "If you could keep him from drinking too much——"

But Christopher was in wild spirits. He was the centre of all the laughter and gaiety and — Stella was egging him on. Karen's lips tightened. In her flame-coloured dress, Stella had looked challenging enough, but with those rather garish emeralds, she looked — exotic, seductive — evil.

It made Karen feel a little sick to watch her until her attention was distracted by something else. Stella was giving Christopher drink after drink. Karen squared her slim shoulders. That at least must be stopped.

She went over to Stella as she stood at the little trolley from which the drinks were being served and said quietly:

"Stella, please don't encourage Christopher to drink so much. It isn't good for him."

Without troubling to turn, Stella shrugged her bare shoulders.

"Don't be a spoil-sport, my child!" she said carelessly.

Karen felt herself go hot with anger.

She deliberately stood in Stella's path.

"Stella, you are being very unkind to Christopher," she said firmly. "As it is, he will have a bad time to-morrow, but if he keeps on drinking it will be a hundred times worse. Surely you can't want to cause him real physical agony?"

Then Stella turned on her, her lips parted to speak. But the words never came for Fred came up at that moment.

"I say, darling," he said, laying his hand on Stella's arm. "Lay off the drinks for Kit! At the rate he's going, he'll be completely out in no time!"

"Oh, rubbish, Fred!" Stella said impatiently, jerking her arm from his gentle clasp. "Kit has always drunk heavily! It won't do him any harm!"

"That was different — when he was a fit man," he insisted, and took the glass from her suddenly unresisting hand. "I can't let you accept the responsibility for encouraging him!"

For a moment Karen thought that Stella was going to resist. Then she shrugged her shoulders and walked off.

For a moment Fred stood regarding the glass in his hand. Then, with a sudden gesture, he tossed the drink off.

"I needed that," he commented and Karen realised that he was speaking as much to himself as to her. Then, with a brief, friendly nod, he went off.

Karen stood quite still. But for Fred's intervention, she knew that nothing would have stopped Stella. For she knew perfectly well that Stella realised just as she did that Christopher was laying up pain and suffering for himself. She knew it and she was deliberately encouraging him to do it. Karen knew. She had seen that momentary gleam of hatred in Stella's eyes and was afraid — for Christopher.

It was two o'clock before the last of the guests went. Christopher insisted on being wheeled out on to the terrace to wave them off. Karen glanced at him covertly. How on earth he had contrived to keep going she could not guess, but a glance at his chalk-white face and the tiny beads of sweat on his forehead showed easily enough to just what strain he had subjected himself.

As they came in again, Stella made for the record player and put on another record. Quite evidently, she had no intention of calling it a day yet. And Christopher, Karen thought, would take up the challenge and refuse to give in.

But she had reckoned without Nature. The drug that Bannister had injected had acted as a stimulant, but gradually its power had decreased and now, suddenly, Christopher reached his limit.

"Push this damned thing into my room," he said thickly. "If I'm going to die, I'd rather do it in my own hole!"

A sudden blight fell on his guests as Bannister hurriedly took command and Karen followed with Fred. Then Stella, who had watched the little scene with a peculiar smile on her lips, shrugged her shoulders.

Deliberately she picked out the noisiest record of the whole collection and put it on.

"Come on," she said holding out her arms invitingly to the nearest man. "It's early yet."

"D'you think we ought?" he asked. "I mean — Kit looked pretty seedy."

"Oh, rubbish!" she said sharply. "Cheer him up a bit!"

But suddenly, from the corridor that led to Kit's room, Karen swept out and switched off the record player. Then she turned round and faced them.

"I'm sorry," she said rather breathlessly, "but there can't be any more music to-night. Kit is — ill. We've sent for the doctor."

There was a little murmur of regret, not untinged with a suggestion of guilt.

"Good heavens! Anyone would think that she really cares for him," Mrs. Denby said out of the corner of her mouth.

"She does, you idiot," Mrs. Cardew said shortly. "And the best thing we can do to help is go to bed and not make too much noise about it." She walked deliberately up to Karen and kissed her. "You poor kid," she murmured under her breath.

There was a general move in the direction of the stairs, but Stella stood her ground.

"My dear," she drawled, "don't you know that the first thing a good hostess learns is that her guests must never be embarrassed by knowing that there is anything wrong. Surely there was a less dramatic way of finishing the party than that!"

"Was there?" Karen said wearily. "I don't know. I — I didn't have time to think. But I'm sure they understood. Kit is really ill, Stella. And quite a lot of it is your fault."

"My dear girl!" Stella's dark eyes opened widely. "What have I done?"

"You know quite well," Karen said quietly. "But if you want to be told — you've spent the evening deliberately exciting Christopher and encouraging him to drink too much."

Stella shrugged and helped herself to a cigarette.

"If you are jealous because I tried to make the party go — a thing of which you are certainly not capable——" she retorted; but Karen interrupted her:

"That just isn't true. Oh about me — yes, perhaps. I'm not a very socially conscious sort of person. But you had no altruistic motives, Stella. You hate Christopher almost as much as you hate me."

"Oh, for goodness' sake, stop calling him Christopher," Stella snapped, stubbing out the cigarette she had just lit. "Everybody calls him Kit."

"If Christopher wants me to call him anything else, he will tell me," Karen told her. "And now, please go upstairs, Stella. We are expecting the doctor and he should be here any minute now."

"How dare you!" Stella suddenly flamed. "How dare you give me orders in Kit's house!"

"In *my* house," Karen said quietly. "You seem to forget, Stella, that I am Christopher's wife."

"I forget nothing," Stella flung at her. "You scheming, money-grabbing little pauper! Oh, it's all very well you pretending to be so upset over Kit, but — don't imagine that people are taken in by it! They know as well as I do that you married him for his money and they are as disgusted as I am! So don't picture yourself a rich widow that everybody is glad to take up because I assure you that they won't!"

Karen looked at her vaguely. She simply hadn't heard what Stella had said because she was listening for the sound of the doctor's car.

"Don't talk so loudly, Stella," she begged. "The house *must* be quiet for Christopher's sake."

"Oh!" Stella said impatiently and ran upstairs. Karen watched her with complete lack of interest. Nothing mattered except Christopher.

The doctor came a few minutes later. Briefly Karen described what had happened during the long and strenuous party that evening, and Dr. Stalham shook his head.

"You ought not to have let him do that, Mrs. Thirlby," he said reproachfully.

"I know that," she admitted. "But — if you know Christopher at all well, you will know just how impossible it is — even now — to persuade him against his will. I think," she added thoughtfully, "perhaps even more now. After all, as far as I can make out, he always has been a dominating personality. Now that he is so helpless, it must give him some sort of satisfaction to compel other people to carry out his wishes."

Dr. Stalham looked at her sharply. He wondered if she had realised just how much she had admitted with her remark, "As far as I can make out." Perhaps she just did not care, he realised, because other things — Christopher — mattered more.

"I'd better see him at once," he said and Karen led the way.

Christopher was lying very rigidly, his eyes fixed on the ceiling above his head, his one good hand gripping a fold in the coverlet.

Dr. Stalham stood looking down at him until he compelled Christopher to meet his eyes. Then, very softly, he said:

"You damned fool!"

He saw Christopher flinch, as he had meant that he should. Then he turned to Karen.

"I'll take over," he said pleasantly. "You run off to bed!"

Karen was about to protest and then she changed her mind. She went slowly upstairs to her bedroom and took off her lovely dress. Carelessly, she threw it over a chair and changed for the night. Then she put on her red housecoat and a pair of sheepskin slippers and went downstairs again to wait in the hall for the doctor to come from Christopher.

It was nearly an hour before he came slowly across the hall to stand beside the fire that she had made up simply for the sake of something to do.

She looked up eagerly but he shook his head.

"It's no good beating about the bush," he said regretfully. "Your husband is very ill indeed. Much worse than he has been any time I have seen him since his accident. In fact, if he goes on like this———" he finished, but Karen's chin went up.

"You mean that he will not even live the six months they said?" she said bravely.

He nodded silently and then said slowly:

"I've got that address for you — the specialist that believes in miracles."

"Yes, of course," Karen said quickly. "We must send for him."

"If your husband will see him," he said, eyes watching her shrewdly. "I'm not at all sure that he will. He's quite convinced that he's going out, you know."

"Oh!" Karen dismissed that with an impatient little gesture. "As if we can take any notice of that now! It is too late to telephone now. But to-morrow morning?"

"All right." Dr. Stalham nodded. "But frankly, unless we get some co-operation out of him———"

"You will," Karen said positively. "You must tell him — the specialist — that Christopher doesn't believe that he has a chance. Though he knows that already, I expect. And as well, both of you must convince Christopher that if he is so reckless, he will end by not being able to move so much as his hand, as he can at present. That he will be utterly dependent on others. You see, it is his loss of independence that he hates worst of all."

Dr. Stalham considered.

"You're a very clever woman," he said slowly. "With a very deep knowledge of human nature."

"Oh no!" Karen shook her head. "It isn't that. It is just that I———" She stopped abruptly and he finished for her.

"That you love your husband so much," he nodded gravely. "I know. Well, I'll do my best to convince Braunton, though I think it will not be very difficult to do that. And now — off you go to bed. I don't want another invalid on my hands!"

Karen smiled crookedly.

"Oh no, that won't happen," she assured him. "I'm — tough, you know. Much more so than I look."

"You're obstinate," he corrected her good-humouredly. "Well, I suppose it's no good wasting my breath. I imagine you intend to stay up all night just in case he wants you?"

"Of course," she said simply.

Dr. Stalham surveyed the sweet, grave face thoughtfully and for the first time saw the strength that was there as well.

"Perhaps you're right," he said slowly. "If anybody can give the poor chap tranquillity of mind — which is his biggest need — it's you!"

Then he left and Karen went slowly to Christopher's rooms. Bannister was just coming out of the inner room and he shook his head when he saw Karen's enquiring eyes.

"He's bad," he said in a whisper. "The doctor gave him a shot of something but it just isn't taking effect. His mind is too active. What are you going to do, madam? He says he doesn't want anybody. He's turned me out."

Karen smiled reassuringly.

"It's all right, Bannister. I am not going to be turned out."

She had got to feel sure of that. If she felt any doubt about her reception, let alone showed it, Christopher would turn her out, too. She must convince him, even as she went into his room, that this was the right place for her to be. And once there, even though he did not recognise it for what it was, she must let him feel the warmth of her love — Christopher who, according to Miss Sarah, had never known love.

He did not move as she went in, perhaps he was not even aware of her presence, for she had been very quiet. Without a word, she drew up a chair beside his bed and took his cold hand in her warm one. Instantly, she felt it stiffen and his lips moved, though she could not hear what he said. But she sat there, silent, waiting. And, at last, his fingers closed round hers.

A little prayer of thankfulness surged through her heart. He had not sent her away. And he was holding on to her. His head turned and she saw the torment in his eyes.

"Don't go!" he whispered.

Karen's clasp tightened.

"Never — so long as you want me."

The minutes ticked by and Karen began to hope that the drug was taking effect when suddenly he said:

"Talk to me — say anything, so long as it stops me thinking!"

"I'm not sure that I know how to talk very well," Karen said thoughtfully. "You see, as far as I can remember, no one has ever imagined that I had anything to say worth while listening to. It comes of living with relatives who are very much older than oneself. Except, of course, the Bungerbies." She laughed softly. "I hadn't thought about them for years. They weren't real, of course. Just a family that I invented. Father, mother and two little Bungerbies. Just neat and tidy like the card game, Happy Families. Mr. Bungerbie was Something in the City. And sometimes he got worried. His chief clerk, Mr. Longbow, was *most* untruthful. Sometimes he would go out to buy stamps and he would not be back for quite half an hour. And then he would say it wasn't his fault because he had had to help an old lady cross the road, and by the time he had put her on her way the time had simply flown. And, of course, Mr. Bungerbie, who was very kind, didn't like to tell him he mustn't help old ladies, but he *did* wish Mr. Longbow would not spend so much time out of the office, because it meant he had to answer the telephone himself and pretend to be someone else, so that clients would not think he was too poor to afford a chief clerk. And he used to tell me all about it and ask my advice. And so did Mrs. Bungerbie. About the children. When they had spots or a slight cold in the head. She was far too much inclined to mollycoddle them," she said severely. She stopped because this childish nonsense might be irritating Christopher beyond endurance, but his clasp tightened and he said, "Go on!" peremptorily.

So, gradually, she unfolded the simple saga of the Bungerbie family and Christopher heard of the Bungerbie's summer holiday, when Karen had helped them with all the preparations and then stayed at home to look after the house in case of burglars; of the time when both Bungerbie children had measles at the same time.

"Very badly, too." Karen assured him seriously. "The spots turned inwards!"

"How did they do that?" Christopher wanted to know.

"I haven't any idea," Karen admitted. "But I heard

someone say it once and it sounded so appalling that I simply had to use it up!"

"Go on!" Christopher was as insatiable as a child for a bedtime story.

He had relaxed, but his eyes were still fixed on her face. Gradually the torment receded and, exultant, Karen believed that he was drawing new strength from her and tirelessly she went on with her story.

Once she thought that she heard Bannister move in the room behind her, but she did not turn, and soon they were alone again together in an odd fantastic world that a lonely little girl had created, only, now, her funny, imaginary family was comforting Christopher. Or she was. It did not matter which.

Suddenly she realised that the grip of his hand had slackened and once, twice, she saw his eyelids droop. She kept on talking, but lowered her voice a little and made it deliberately sing-song. Again his eyes closed — and this time they did not open again. Christopher was asleep.

Karen watched his sleeping face. He looked so much younger like this. And so vulnerable. Her lips curved tenderly. At that moment, she felt as if she had achieved her heart's desire. She had stood between Christopher and the devils that tormented him.

Then, because she was very tired, she put her head down on the bed beside the hand she held and fell asleep herself.

CHAPTER SEVEN

AT first when Karen woke up she could not remember where she was. The sun was peeping in from an unusual angle and she could hear the soft breathing of someone else.

Then she remembered. Cautiously she lifted her head and looked at Christopher's sleeping face. With a catch at the heart, she saw how young he looked. She had thought that the previous night but there was something additional now — there was a degree of tranquillity about his expression that surely meant something rather important. Life simply must be easier for him, however much or little of it there might be left to him, if he could stop living on his nerves, stop living for the sake of hatred. And it seemed to her that some of the hatred must have seeped out of him or he simply could not look like that.

Her hand was still lying in his, but only in such a light clasp that it was possible for her to draw away without disturbing him. But when she tried to get up, she almost fell forward. She had not realised how stiff and cramped she was through sleeping in that strained position. With an effort, she righted herself and tiptoed to the outer room.

Bannister was asleep in an armchair, his collar and tie off and his shirt opened at the neck. His thin hair was disarranged and involuntarily Karen smiled at the comparison his appearance made to his usual immaculate state. She thought compassionately:

"Poor Bannister. He must be dreadfully tired and yet he never complains!" That was because, in his way, he loved Christopher, just as she did. She walked softly to the outer-door, hoping that she need not disturb him, but she must have made a slight sound, for Bannister, used to being on the alert for Christopher, was suddenly on his feet.

"Oh, I'm so sorry, Bannister!" she said regretfully. "I didn't want to wake you up."

"It's quite all right, madam," he said, mechanically smoothing his hair. And then, he glanced at the clock: "Good heavens! Is that the time?"

"Half-past seven," Karen said. "Yes, it must be. Look at the sunshine."

"Mr. Christopher?" Bannister said anxiously.

"He is still asleep," Karen told him thankfully.

Bannister gave a little exclamation.

"Then he's had over four hours' sleep," he said in amazement. "That's the longest he's had since his accident! Did you give him anything, madam? The doctor left some pills, though I'm afraid I forgot to tell you."

"He didn't need them," Karen said, trying to suppress a yawn. "We just talked — I think he forgot about himself."

Bannister looked as if he were struggling to express an emotion at which Karen could easily guess, but apparently his sense of the conventions came to his aid and his gratitude showed itself in a little suggestion that he should make a cup of tea.

"Oh, could you, Bannister?" she said longingly. "Let's both have one!"

Five minutes later they were sitting either side of the electric fire drinking thirstily, and Karen almost choked with laughter at the thought of what Stella would say if she could see them! The mistress of the house in a dressing-gown and the manservant without a collar and tie sharing an early morning cup of tea! Well, it might not be the way to treat ordinary servants, but then Bannister was not ordinary. Karen leaned forward.

"Bannister," she said earnestly. "I want you to watch Mr. Christopher closely this morning. For the tiniest of little differences. I think he looks — well, you see what you think."

"Yes, madam." Bannister watched her alertly. Like the rest of Christopher's staff, he knew just what was going on, and though he held himself strictly aloof from gossip, it did not prevent him from having his own opinions. If it had turned out that Lady Thirlby had married his master instead of Sir Frederick, well, he'd have accepted the situation, but more than once he had wondered just how it would have worked out. Now this nice little girl——

"Dr. Stalham is bringing Mr. Braunton, the specialist, down to see Christopher this afternoon," she went on. "What time do you think most of our guests will go?"

"I think if they've any sort of feeling, they'll go first thing after breakfast," Bannister said with sudden heat. "After the way they went on last night."

"It wasn't exactly their fault," Karen said mechanically. "At least——" She stopped herself, realisig that she must not criticise Stella to Bannister.

"Of course," he went on carefully, "probably Sir Frederick and Lady Thirlby will stay on — that was arranged beforehand, I understand. So that Sir Frederick could look after things that need attention on the estate."

"Yes," Karen said and no amount of caution could prevent the note of regret in her voice. She stood up and so did Bannister.

"I am going to telephone to Cullen at the lodge," she said. "I want him to stand right at the end of the corridor with" — she glanced round the room at the trophies hung on the wall — "with that battle axe. And if anybody tries to disturb Mr. Christopher, he is to kill them. As quietly as possible, of course."

"Quite, madam," Bannister said gravely and approvingly. "I myself will sit at the window of this room and if anybody approaches, I will deal with them!"

"I am sure you will," Karen said gratefully. "I will tell one of the maids to bring you breakfast, Bannister. She can put it through the window as well, and then the door need not be opened unnecessarily."

"Thank you, madam." He watched her retreating figure with approval. A real lady, that, whatever her origin. Not always worrying about what people might think, but just relying on her own good sense. And knowing that it was her duty to see that her servants were well looked after. Bannister sighed.

If only there was a little more hope that Mr. Christopher would get well, he'd soon find out what a treasure he'd married!

Bannister was right. Without exception, all the visitors made quiet farewells to Karen and had left the house by eleven o'clock.

Mrs. Cardew kissed her warmly as she left.

"Now, listen to me," she said earnestly, if enigmatically.

"Don't you take anything from anybody that you don't want to! Remember, you're the mistress here and — stick to your guns!" She limped away before Karen could reply, but her friendliness left a warm little glow in her heart.

Stella had not come down to breakfast.

"She's got a bit of a headache," Fred explained rather anxiously. "A rum thing for her. She's got an amazing constitution, as a rule. I've known her dance till six in the morning and then ride to hounds at nine looking as fresh as a daisy. Of course, the fact of it is," he said confidentially to his cousin's wife, "She has always been very fond of Kit — I told you the three of us have always been tremendous pals — and it upsets her to see him like this." He hesitated and cleared his throat. "That's why she was — well, a bit hysterical last night. You understood that, didn't you?"

"Oh yes, of course," Karen said gently, understanding quite well that he was trying to reassure himself rather than her.

He smiled in evident relief.

"Now tell me what your plans are."

He nodded approvingly when she explained, and after a minute's pause asked tentatively:

"Karen — do you think Kit has got a Chinaman's chance?"

Karen bit her lips to keep back the tears.

"Fred, he must have — he shall have!" she said passionately. "I — I can't let him go!"

"You poor kid!" Fred said compassionately and put a kindly arm round her.

Just for a minute Karen rested her dark head against his friendly, tweed-clad shoulder.

"Oh, Fred, he's all I've got!" she murmured brokenly.

"You poor kid!" he said again.

Stella, who had been on the point of entering the room, softly withdrew. She had heard quite clearly what had been said. But she had also seen the reflection of her husband and that interloping girl in a mirror on the opposite wall.

Her expression was very thoughtful as she went slowly upstairs again. How different, she was thinking, things could appear to be from what they actually were in fact!

The doctor and the specialist arrived during the morning and, after an anxious hour during which Karen waited in the outer room, the two men came out.

Karen stood up, her grey eyes fixed on the man who held the secret of Christopher's future in his hands.

Forster Braunton waited until the door was firmly shut between the two rooms, then he said quietly:

"There are some people, Mrs. Thirlby, whom I might try to comfort with specious vagueness. But not you. I am going to tell you the absolute truth."

"Yes," she breathed, her heart sinking, yet finding comfort in his frankness.

"And the truth is this. I cannot possibly tell you what your husband's chances are."

"But he still has a chance?" she asked steadily.

For a moment he pursed his lips.

"If I was right in saying that he had a chance to begin with — and I believe that I was — then he still has. In fact——" He hesitated again. "Frankly, Mrs. Thirlby, I am reluctant to raise your hopes too much, but undeniably it is a miracle that, after what has happened, he is not in a far worse condition than he is."

Karen's heart gave a little leap, but she deliberately held herself in check.

"He was very bad last night," she said reluctantly. "Worse than I have ever seen him."

"So I understand." Forster Braunton nodded. "Now, Mrs. Thirlby, in your opinion was the cause of that condition mental or physical?"

"Partly physical," she said promptly. "He had been propped up far too high and he was obviously in pain. But mainly it was mental exhaustion, I think. I'm sure that all this week, having people here has brought his own helplessness to him and, besides that——" She stopped. Not unless it was absolutely essential could she tell either of these men, kind though they were, about that horrible desire for revenge that Christopher had hugged to himself. Choosing her words very carefully, she said slowly: "There are special reasons why his accident has made him very bitter. This party was a sort of defiance against — things. And — I think he realises that — that he can't *make* things happen the way he used to any more. Last night he did not want to think about himself or his old life. He only wanted to forget."

"His man tells me that it was owing to you that he had quite a good sleep," Dr. Stalham said curiously. "What did you give him, Mrs. Thirlby?"

"Nothing. I told him tales." Karen said simply. "And held his hand. That's all."

"If you remember, I told you that you, if anybody, could give him tranquillity of mind," Dr. Stalham interjected approvingly. "You could not have done better."

Karen flushed at his praise and then turned gravely to the other man.

"What must we do?" she asked. "Is there nothing that can be done to help?"

"Yes," he said thoughtfully. "I think that there is. Again, I cannot say whether it will be successful or not, but your husband is in a far more receptive frame of mind than when I saw him before. He is willing to experiment. Dr. Stalham is arranging for a masseur to come over three times a week. We are going to start on his other hand and arm. And I want you and his man, without letting him realise it, to watch all the time for the slightest of voluntary movements even of the little finger of that hand. Moreover, I want you to give him things so that it would be more convenient for him to take them left-handed. Do you understand? There may be no response, almost certainly not at first. But sooner or later he may, unconsciously, make a movement simply because it is convenient to do so. You see, we have got to break down his conviction that he will never be any better. His agreement to have treatment is a great step forward. It may lead to others. But — there must be no more excitement such as there has been this week. And no more excessive drinking. But I do not think you need worry about that. As a matter of fact, I took your advice, Mrs. Thirlby. I told him that to continue that way meant complete dependence on others. You know your husband well! He reacted exactly as we could wish! And now I must hurry off! Dr. Stalham will keep in touch with

108

me, but if you wish to do so as well, please do not hesitate! And — good luck to both of you!"

Karen saw the two men off and then she went in to Christopher.

He was lying very still and he looked tired, but she realised that the examination he had had would account for that. She came very quietly to his side and took his hand in hers as she had done the night before, and again his fingers closed over hers. For a moment neither of them spoke. Then Christopher said slowly without looking at her:

"In a way, it was easier when I believed that in six months' time I should be dead. It put a period to it all. Now — there is uncertainty. I'm not sure that isn't harder."

"You faced the other by yourself," she reminded him gently. "This — we can share."

Christopher's head turned slowly on the pillow and their eyes met. It seemed to Karen that all the love, all the tenderness she had for him rushed towards him and surely, she thought, he must *see* it. But if he did, there was no responding spark in his own eyes. He just drew a deep, sighing breath and turned away again. But his hand still held hers and she stood there quietly waiting, until, with another little sigh, Christopher seemed to relax and she knew that he was sleeping. She waited until his grasp slackened and released herself. But she could not go. For a long time she stood there watching him, studying every line of the strong, arrogant face. Then, greatly daring, she stooped and gently touched the crisp hair with her lips.

She went to find Fred with a lightened heart. There was, despite Mr. Braunton's caution, more grounds for hope than there had been. And she could help!

Christopher did not love her. She had no illusions about that. But because she loved him, he could draw strength and comfort from her, even though he might not understand why. She almost hoped that he never would. For then he would accept all that she could give without question as a child might and she would have that utter joy of love, giving to the beloved. She asked no more.

Life settled down into an ordered routine which, to Karen's relief, Christopher seemed to accept quite willingly.

The masseur came three times a week, and fortunately Bannister, jealously alert where Christopher was concerned, took to him. These visits left Christopher somewhat tired, but grimly cheerful. All the effort that he had previously put into planning for the house party and later entertaining his guests, he now seemed to be putting into this new resolution to give himself every chance of recovery if that were possible.

Fred's own smaller estate was only a few miles away, and though it kept him very busy he managed to run Christopher's as well as his own. Everything he did was first discussed with Christopher if that were possible, and if not, was later reported to him with meticulous care. It was almost as if Fred were determined to show that he was acting purely as his cousin's agent and not as if, at one time, he had been his heir.

Whatever his reason, everything went smoothly, and Karen found herself feeling happier than she had ever done in her life.

Stella was the one fly in the ointment and actually even she hardly disturbed the tranquil tenor of life at Claverings. Most of her time was spent either in her own room or out visiting old friends. Such time as she spent with the others was usually during the evening and she seemed to have accepted the necessity for quietness, for she rarely talked much.

As a matter of fact, Stella had a lot to think about. Quite frankly, to herself, she admitted that she had acted too precipitately in marrying Fred. She ought to have gambled on the future and her own luck. For now, it appeared, there was, after all, a chance that Kit might live. Not a very good chance, perhaps, but previously there had been none at all.

Which was it going to be? If he was, after all, going to die, then somehow or other, she must discredit Karen with Kit. Then there would be a good chance of him altering his will back to its original terms. In that case, she must contrive to tolerate life with Fred, boring though it was.

But if Kit was not, after all, going to die, then just how much better would he get? If he was going to be a hopeless invalid, then she must just cut her losses and stick to

110

Fred. But supposing he was going to get completely well!

That was the possibility that intrigued Stella. Her eyes narrowed speculatively. That little scene she had watched unknown to Fred and Karen had put an idea into her head that slowly bore fruit. Supposing one wanted to get rid of both Fred and Karen. What better way could there be of doing it than by linking their names? If they could be compromised——

It would not be easy. She realised that. But — she would have Kit on her side. She smiled as she reflected that in trying to revenge himself on her, he had admitted just how much she mattered to him. His marriage had been for one purpose only — suppose he found himself a completely fit man with this little nonentity tied to him for life? Wouldn't he be only too glad to be shown a way of getting rid of her and of marrying, instead, the girl whom he always wanted to — herself?

But she mustn't rush things. For one thing, she did not yet know just what was going to happen. But whatever plan she carried out, they all had one thing in common. She must discredit Karen. And it was not so easy. There was no doubt about it, the girl was quite a good nurse, and in the present circumstances that gave her an unquestioned advantage. And Kit seemed to accept her everlasting presence in his room as a matter of course.

It was Fred who, all unintentionally, gave her a valuable hint.

"I say, darling," he said one night as they were preparing for bed. "There's something I wish you would do."

Stella, without pausing in the steady brushing of her hair, gave a quick glance to Fred's reflection in her mirror. She did not feel particularly like falling in with any of Fred's wishes at the moment, yet some instinct warned her to be gracious — an instinct which she afterwards realised had served her in good stead.

"If I can," she said amiably but noncommittally.

Fred came and stood behind her, and, taking up a strand of her hair, twisted it round his finger.

"It's about Karen," he said thoughtfully.

"Karen?" Stella could not keep a sharp note out of her voice. "What's the matter with her?"

"She's not looking too fit," Fred pursued, conscious that, as so often, he had annoyed Stella without understanding why. "Haven't you noticed how pale she is?"

"Oh, that's her natural colouring," Stella said carelessly. "Most of us would look washed out if we didn't use make-up. And she doesn't. Actually, something of an affectation these days when absolutely everyone does."

"Yes; I know that," Fred admitted. "But I'm comparing her with what she was a few weeks ago. Fact of the matter is, she's not getting out enough! Of course, it's natural enough for her to want to spend all the time she can with poor old Kit, particularly as she's certainly got the knack of keeping him quiet." He paused and hastily dismissed the wish that had come unbidden into his head that Stella would be a bit more understanding and kindly. Such a thought, to Fred, was utter disloyalty. "You know what Kit has always been," he went on half apologetically. "A beggar for getting what he wants, regardless of other people's feelings."

"Do you mean to say he *wants* Karen bossing him all the time?" she asked incredulously.

"I don't think she bosses him," Fred said carefully. "I'm quite sure he wants her with him, but the whole thing is, it just doesn't occur to him that it isn't good for Karen never to get a break and she's much too sweet ever to tell him so."

"Is she?" Stella spoke thoughtfully. Her own opinion was that Karen was more than capable of looking after herself, but she had suddenly realised what Fred was driving at. "What do you think we ought to do about it?"

"Well, what I wondered was, would you offer to spend a bit more time with Kit so that she could go out? I could teach her to ride or something."

Stella suppressed a little laugh of triumph. But how quite perfect! Fred, in the kindness of his heart, obligingly slipping his head into the noose and holding it open for Karen to do the same.

"I think you are right in principle," she said slowly. "And I am perfectly willing to do my share. But I don't think that I am the right person to suggest it. You see, for one thing Karen doesn't like me very much. I can't think why," she added regretfully. "For I've gone out of my way to be nice to her. But there it is. The other thing is that, quite obviously, Karen thinks it is her duty to stay with Kit, and I don't think she is going to be persuaded that it isn't by anybody like us. Now, if you had a word in confidence with Dr. Stalham——"

"Yes, of course!" Fred stooped and, tipping her head gently back, kissed her white forehead. "I might have known you'd see the way it ought to be done! I'll drop in on Stalham to-morrow morning at his house. Then Karen won't even know the idea originated from us. Though that seems a bit underhanded," he finished distastefully.

"It does in a way," Stella admitted gravely. "But the way that we have got to look at it is this: Karen needs looking after and this appears to be the only way that we can do it. In any case, Dr. Stalham won't say anything unless *he* thinks it is necessary. You see, you'll only be calling his attention to what you feel is the situation. If he doesn't think it is——"

"Yes; of course." Fred sighed with relief. "Bless you, Stella. You're a dear, understanding soul!"

Stella smiled sweetly as she began to cream her face. Fred was a dull bore and Stella wanted excitement and entertainment from life. And she intended to have them; if not one way, then another.

Dr. Stalham was quick to confirm Fred's impression.

"Thirlby is a selfish devil," he commented. "And his wife is as sweet a girl as I've ever come across. How he had the good sense to marry her — particularly as I'd always thought he was going to—— Well, that doesn't matter now," he finished hastily, suddenly remembering that Fred had married the girl everyone had forecast would be Mrs. Christopher Thirlby. "Yes; I'll certainly see what I can do about it."

But he found it difficult to get Karen to listen.

"Really, I'm quite all right," she insisted. "And, besides, Christopher needs me."

"You're quite right; he does," Dr. Stalham agreed bluffly. "That's the whole point, Mrs. Christopher. Don't you see, I simply can't have you breaking down, because, if you do, I just can't say what the effect will be on your husband."

"But I shan't break down." All the same, in spite of confident words, he heard a faint note of doubt in her tone and proceeded to make the most of it.

"I'm not proposing that you should go away or anything like that," he went on. "Because, though that might do you good in one way, I know perfectly well that you'd be worrying yourself really ill wondering how your husband was. But — the odd half hour here and there — surely you can manage that?"

"Yes, I suppose I can," she admitted.

"Well, then — I'll have a word with him about it."

Karen looked startled.

"With Christopher? But why? Don't you think it would be better if he didn't know? You see," she went on earnestly, "it would be dreadful if he began to think that he was being a burden to me. And he isn't — he isn't!"

"Yes; perhaps so," he admitted. "Well, it rests with you. If you're sensible about this, there will be no need to say anything. But if not, then I shall have to see that your husband looks after you better."

He spoke lightly and was unprepared for the tears that sprang to her eyes.

"Oh, Dr. Stalham, how can you expect him to!" she protested. "It must take him all the strength he's got to get through each day as it is, without worrying about how other people feel."

"That's where you're wrong," he told her. "The more he thinks about other people the better, because it means that he thinks less about his own condition. It would do him all the good in the world to worry about you."

"But you don't understand——" she began and stopped. After all, how could she explain to the doctor that, though she loved Christopher with all her being, his feeling for her was nothing more than that of a patient for a nurse he can trust? Oh, perhaps it was a little more than that now. Perhaps he felt a certain amount of affection — but that was a very different matter from loving her. "I'll be sensible," she promised, smiling at the doctor reassuringly.

Fred was delighted at Karen's willingness to listen to the doctor and promptly suggested that she should ride with him.

"But I have never been on a horse in my life," she protested laughingly. "Except a wooden one on a roundabout! Besides, I haven't any clothes for it."

"Oh, Stella will lend you some," Fred suggested easily. "Won't you, Stella?"

"But of course," Stella agreed amiably. "That is, if Karen does not mind wearing my clothes?"

Karen hesitated momentarily. It was obvious to her if not to Fred, that Stella knew perfectly well that she hated the idea of using anything that belonged to the girl who had treated Christopher so heartlessly. But that was something that it was impossible to say in front of Fred.

"But won't that mean you can't come?" Karen suggested.

Stella, quick to realise that she must do nothing to scare Karen now that she had got so far with her plan, shook her head.

"Oh no; I have two outfits here," she said casually. "If I wanted to come. But I don't think I will to-day. For one thing, it is better for a beginner only to have one instructor, and for another, I want to go and see Aunt Sarah."

Karen gave a little sigh of relief. She knew perfectly well that she did need to get out more, but the thought of going out with Fred and so leaving Stella free to spend as much time with Christopher as she liked, had frightened her a little. Still — if Stella was going to be out as well——

Secretly, she was rather frightened, too, at the thought of riding. A horse looked so huge, she thought, and it was with considerable relief that she saw the leading rein which Fred held. He laughed at her change of expression.

"It's a good job old Dolly can't read faces," he commented. "Otherwise she might be tempted to lead you a dance for sheer cussedness. Actually, she's a perfect lamb, and in a week or two you'll be telling me that you want something with a bit more spirit!"

"I hope so!" Karen said doubtfully as she let him help her scramble rather ungracefully on to the mare's broad back.

Stella sauntered with them as far as the field that Fred

had chosen for Karen's first lesson, and then took the turning that led to Miss Sarah's house. She did not look forward in the least to the visit, knowing the old lady's caustic tongue of old, but she was philosophic about it. It served her purpose and consequently was worth putting up with.

Miss Sarah opened the door herself.

"Well, this is an honour!" she commented caustically.

"Rather a belated one, I am afraid," Stella said sweetly. "But we have been rather busy up at Claverings."

"So I understand," Miss Sarah said, standing aside for her visitor to pass. "How is the boy now?"

Stella shrugged her shoulders.

"No one seems to know," she replied, her smooth forehead furrowed as if she were really troubled. "It is rather — worrying."

"Why?" Miss Sarah asked bluntly. "No particular business of yours, is it? After all, you saw to it that it wasn't, didn't you?"

There was murder in Stella's heart for this shrewd old woman who, without knowing the truth, had none the less guessed it. But only bewilderment was expressed in her lovely face.

"I don't quite understand," she said hesitatingly. And then drew her breath in sharply. "You don't mean — you don't think I married Fred because Kit was hurt, do you?" she demanded anxiously.

Miss Sarah shrugged her ample shoulders.

"Didn't you?" she asked noncommittally.

Stella shook her head.

"No; I didn't. Although, of course, I've realised that some ungenerous people were bound to imagine something like that. Actually, the news about Kit did not reach us until we had been married some days."

Miss Sarah regarded her searchingly.

"Something of a coincidence that you were married the very day that Christopher crashed, wasn't it?" she suggested, obviously a little less sure of herself.

Stella shrugged her shoulders.

"But coincidences do happen," she pointed out smilingly. "Oh, I know you've always been prejudiced against me, Aunt Sarah. But — try to look at it from my point of view.

116

It is perfectly true that both Kit and Fred wanted to ⌐ ⌐ me. Well, you know Kit. He's fascinating and exciting — no girl could help being flattered and I admit that I was no exception. But — you see, I asked him not to fly that day and he simply laughed. He wanted to, and that was what mattered. And, suddenly, I realised just what life with him would mean. Aunt Sarah," she said earnestly, "can you deny that Fred is kinder and more thoughtful than Kit? Or that a woman's happiness will be safer in his hands?"

"No," Miss Sarah admitted grudgingly. "That's true enough. But I didn't think that you were the sort of girl who worried about safety and common sense. I thought you were just such another as Christopher himself."

"Women get over that sort of thing sooner than men do," Stella pointed out with some truth. "And I have."

"So you married Fred," Miss Sarah concluded.

"So I married Fred," Stella agreed. "Do you blame me?"

Miss Sarah shrugged her shoulders.

"My dear girl, I rarely blame anybody. There is so little need to. If you've done the right thing, then so much the better. If you haven't, then you'll be the one that pays, believe me! And now, if you'll excuse me, I've got a job to do. Stay by all means if you like, but I don't suppose you will enjoy watching me clean out the chicken-house, much less help."

Stella went back to Claverings by an alternative route, so that Fred and Karen did not see her, and went up to her room. She took off her fur coat and cap, repaired her make-up and combed her hair and then went quietly down to Christopher's room.

Bannister was not there and Kit appeared to be sleeping. For a moment she stood watching him, an inscrutable expression on her face. Then, quite deliberately, she pushed a book off the table beside him.

Christopher awoke with a little jerk.

"Karen——" he began. Then, fully awake, he saw that it was not Karen but Stella. He frowned. "I want Karen," he said bluntly.

Stella hesitated, very obviously embarrassed.

"Well, what is it?" he demanded.

Again Stella hesitated.

"You're putting me in rather a difficult position, Kit," she said diffidently. "You see, Karen asked me not to tell you——"

"Tell me what?" he insisted. "Go on. You've gone so far. You'd better tell me the whole story."

"Oh but it's nothing, really," she insisted. "In fact, I thought it was all rather unnecessary. It's only that Karen asked Fred to teach her to ride and they are out now."

"Teach her to——?" She saw the frustration and pain in his face and knew that she was on the point of achieving the effect she wanted.

"Oh, Kit I know!" she said, gently touching his hand. "It must hurt you! But — try to see it from her point of view! She has never had any luxuries in her life and now — she is surrounded by them. Is it unreasonable that she should want to make use of her opportunities?"

"No," he admitted. "I suppose not."

"And you must admit," she went on, watching him closely, "that she has been very tactful. She insisted that you were not to be told."

His face darkened with fury.

"My God! What does she think I am?" he demanded violently. "I may be a helpless log, but I'm neither a child nor a dog-in-the-manger! Tell her to come to me the minute she comes in — without changing!"

"Yes, of course, Kit," Stella said, triumph in her heart.

A quarter of an hour later, Karen stood beside him, flushed with her exercise in the chilly air and looking lovelier than anyone who had known her old, pale self would have believed possible.

"I'm so sorry, Christopher," she said breathlessly.

He interrupted her with an impatient little gesture.

"But why should you be?" he asked icily. "I thought you quite understood that you are the mistress of the house and consequently in a position to make any decisions you see fit. If you want to ride, ride. Why not! But in future, please be sensible about it. I know perfectly well that you married me for what you could get out of it so you don't need to be so infernally tactful about it. I'm not a spoilt child!"

That, of course, was just exactly what he was, but how could one tell him so?

"But that wasn't the reason——" she began and again he silenced her.

"Wasn't it?" he said shortly. "Well, it seems the most obvious one to me!"

Karen said nothing. After all, what could she say? Her decision not to say anything to him had been made in all good faith, and it had never occurred to her that her action was capable of an entirely different interpretation — and not a very pleasant one at that. She could, of course, tell him the truth, that she had fallen in with the doctor's suggestion because she knew that she was beginning to feel the strain of caring for Christopher. But that was the last thing that she wanted to do, so she stood there silent.

"Well?" Christopher said shortly.

"I'll remember in future," Karen said quietly and went out.

She walked slowly up the stairs, hurt, apprehensive and sick at heart. And Stella, watching her despondent figure, smiled faintly. It really was too easy!

CHAPTER EIGHT

THERE were dark circles round Karen's eyes when she came down to breakfast the next morning. Stella had elected to have her breakfast in bed.

Fred greeted her cheerfully and helped her to bacon and eggs from the covered dish.

"Not too much, Fred," she said smiling rather crookedly. "I don't feel very much like eating this morning."

Fred patted her shoulder kindly as he went back to his own seat.

"Are you still worrying about yesterday?" he asked diffidently and Karen nodded in silence. "I shouldn't too much, if I were you. I mean—it just got under Kit's skin for the time being, but then people who aren't well are like that. He'll forget."

"Perhaps," Karen said without much conviction. She sighed regretfully. "Oh, Fred, I honestly thought I was doing the right thing, but now, of course, I realise that it did look as if I were doing something behind his back. And yet I couldn't explain. But I have made up my mind what I shall do in future," she went on. "I shall take him at his word—make the decisions that I think are right just as I should if he were well. Otherwise I am just rubbing in all the time the fact that he isn't well."

"Something in that," Fred said judicially. "All the same, I don't suppose you feel very keen on riding any more, do you?"

"To be perfectly honest, I don't," Karen admitted. "And not only because of Christopher. But I *must* ride again because I'm frightened to. And I've got to the point where I mustn't let myself be frightened of anything. When I realised that *I* had ridden that great, terrifying brute——" She stopped because Fred was roaring with laughter.

"You funny kid! I told you, Old Dolly is more like an armchair than a horse! You were as safe as houses!"

"I expect I was. My inside self tells me that I was," she admitted. "But all the same—I don't suppose you can quite understand, because you have always ridden, haven't you?"

"Lord, yes. Almost as soon as I could walk," he agreed. "Yes, I suppose it does make a difference. What time, then?"

Karen wrinkled her forehead in thought.

"The masseur comes at eleven. I could come out for an hour. I think I'll go and see Christopher now—and tell him."

"Are you going to tell him why you're so keen on keeping on?" Fred asked curiously. "After all, Stalham will back you up!"

She shook her head vigorously.

"Oh no; I couldn't do that!" she said emphatically. "Don't you see, it's better that I should let him think the way he does now than that he should realise how—how tired I get sometimes."

Fred said nothing. He was genuinely fond of his cousin, but there were times when he wished to goodness that circumstances didn't keep him from telling him what a selfish devil he was where Karen was concerned. Still, if he couldn't do that, at least he could do his best to cheer the little girl up!

Karen went over to Christopher's quarters, but she paused for a minute by the big hall window. Almost imperceptibly the year had crept on, and now it was December. From this window, through a dip in the Downs, she could just see the glint of sunshine on the sea, and all the land between was Christopher's. Involuntarily she sighed. If Christopher were well and strong, if it was with him that she was going riding this morning instead of Fred, what a perfect world it would be! But as it was, all this land, this beautiful house and all the possessions that she shared with him were dust and ashes to both of them—

She checked a litle sob and went into Christopher's room.

He was reading and he did not put the book down as she came in, as he usually did.

"Good morning, Christopher!"

He laid the book down, but kept his place with one

finger, as though he could hardly wait to pick it up again.

"Good morning, Karen," he said in a tone so impersonally polite that it seemed as if he were talking to a stranger.

"I wondered if there was anything that you wanted in the village," she said hesitatingly, uncertain how to deal with this new mood of his.

"Nothing, thank you," he said remotely, half lifting his book again.

Her resolution to behave naturally with him suddenly collapsed like a punctured balloon. She could neither find anything to say nor could she contrive to move from where she stood.

"Is there anything else you wanted to say?" asked the polite, impersonal voice.

"No—except that I am going riding with Fred again while Mr. Louden is with you."

"A good idea," he said carelessly. "You'd better order some jodhpurs. Have them properly tailored."

"Very well, Christopher," she said quietly, and he picked up his book again.

It was an unmistakable dismissal and she had no choice but to leave him.

As he heard the door latch behind her, Christopher laid down his book again. For a long time he lay staring fixedly at the ceiling, his face a set mask, his lips a thin, tense line.

The treatment that Christopher was having was, in one way, disappointing. He did not seem to regain any use of his left arm or hand. On the other hand, there was no doubt but that his general health was better, and after a week or so Dr. Stalham suggested that he should spend less of his time in his own room and more with other people.

"Only, mind, no more wild parties," he warned bluntly. "Your wife and your cousins and perhaps the odd visitor. Understand?"

"Oh, quite," Kit said savagely. "I realise that the only way for me to keep on living is to behave in a way that makes it not worth while doing! Why the devil you couldn't have put me out to begin with——"

"It might have been better," Dr. Stalham said acidly.

"The only trouble is that you would not have been here to take the responsibility. And I've no intention of hanging to save you bother."

Christopher said nothing, but when Karen came to see him after the doctor had gone, he gave her a smile that made her heart leap.

"Will it be much bother if I spend the evening in the lounge?" he asked. "I mean, this couch takes up quite a bit of room."

"It will be quite all right if I have the other couch moved to the back of the room," she said reassuringly.

She went about that day with a light heart. Surely, surely, Christopher was going to get better! He must do! Surely her own deep, passionate longing would compel it to happen!

It was not until the evening that she realised that whereas when Christopher spent the evening in his own room, Stella and Fred rarely came there, they naturally all shared the lounge. And Stella was in a mood which was quite strange to Karen.

For Stella it had been perfectly obvious that her stab about Karen wanting to enjoy the wealth with which she was surrounded had hit Kit hard. So Stella was in a good mood and found it to be little exertion to be both charming and entertaining for Kit's benefit.

She had a gift, which she rarely troubled to exercise, of making the little day-to-day incidents of life sound amusing, and if that was because she did not hesitate both to delete fact and add finishing touches from her imagination, well, no one was likely to criticise even if they could check up on her, because everybody likes to be amused.

Her description of an interview between Miss Sarah and her gardener had both Fred and Christopher laughing.

"You see, they were at loggerheads over how and where the bulbs were to go," Stella explained with a quick side glance at Karen. "And, talking about Aunt Sarah, Kit, what are you going to do about Christmas?"

"Christmas?" he frowned and shrugged his shoulders. "What can I do—like this?"

"Oh, of course, not the usual sort of thing," Stella said quickly. "But you could invite the Pilbrights and Aunt

Sarah. Not very gay, but, still, they expect it, and really they are quite amusing. And the children's party, of course."

"Oh Lord, I'd forgotten that," Christopher said wearily. "Yes, of course they must have their party." He looked doubtfully at Karen.

"Mrs. Paynton was talking to me about that this morning," she said promptly. "She gave me the lists from last year and I was going to ask you about it. She says that she can manage the food side of it all right and suggested that I should ask the Rector to help me get the list up to date."

Stella bit her lip. She had assumed that Karen knew nothing of the annual party that had become a tradition at Claverings, and it was rather annoying that Mrs. Paynton had brought the matter up. As a matter of fact, it frequently did annoy Stella to see how most of the servants were, as she put it, under Karen's thumb.

"Oh, good." Christopher glanced at Fred. "Afraid you'll have to be Santa Claus this year, old man," he said ruefully. "Still, it's all in the family; that's one thing."

"And the presents?" Stella said softly. She had no particular desire to go up to Town and spend a wearisome and boring day choosing gifts for wretched little village children, but it was too good an opportunity to miss.

Karen's lips parted, but before she could speak out Christopher replied.

"Would you mind taking that on, Stella?" he asked. "I mean, you know the sort of thing that we always have."

"Yes, of course, Kit dear," Stella said softly. "You know I would do anything to help. And to save Karen bother."

Karen said nothing because there seemed nothing that could be said without making her appear ungracious, but Christopher's quick frown told her that her silence had been the wrong thing. She gave a little sigh. So often Stella did say things like that which left one floundering between two stools. She had simply not wanted to seem unpleasant to Stella, but the result was that to Chrisopher it must look as if she were glad to be saved the bother.

Keyed up and acutely sensitive as she was these days, it seemed to her that the more cheerful mood in which

Christopher had been gradually left him from that minute. Stella, however, seemed to notice nothing and kept up her cheerful, light-hearted chatter that always contrived to leave Karen on the fringes of the conversation with nothing to say.

And Fred, delighted at seeing old Kit so much more cheery, was none the less troubled at seeing Karen sitting there so quiet and left out of it. He exerted his own not very considerable powers of conversation and Karen turned to him eagerly. Karen realised gratefully that she now knew almost as much of the routine which the party always followed to be able to play her part without disaster. Stella realised it as well and deliberately cut across the conversation. She was not going to let Fred, with his usual muddle-headed good nature, spoil her plans if she could help it.

"Fred!" she said softly and then, as he did not notice, she turned to Christopher. "My husband and your wife seem to be too absorbed in their own conversation to notice us," she said laughingly. "Fred!"

"My dear! Yes," he said quickly.

"What about some drinks?" she suggested. "Oh, I know," she added impatiently, as she saw Fred's doubtful glance at Christopher. "But the odd one is all right, isn't it, Kit?"

"Of course it is," he said impatiently. "Yes; ring for them, Fred!"

Karen, unaccustomed as she was to drinks of any sort, had never succeeded in being able to take more than one—and even to drink that meant a struggle not to let the unaccustomed taste wry her face. She realised, of course, that other people—Fred and Stella, for example—could take far more than that without it doing them the least bit of harm. And Christopher had, no doubt, always been used to the same standards as they were. But things were different now and her face grew troubled as, without question, Stella or Fred refilled his glass several times.

She came and stood by Christopher and spoke very quietly so that the others would hardly be likely to hear what she said.

"Christopher, please do remember what Dr. Stalham said—about drinking, I mean."

There was a little silence across which Stella's light

laugh, tinkling like a little bell, broke. More than likely she was laughing at something that Fred had said and it had nothing to do with Christopher or Karen, but it had the effect of ridicule directed at both of them.

Christopher flushed darkly and made an impatient movement of his hand.

"I wonder," he said coldly and deliberately, "if you could possibly get it into your head that I did not marry you for you to be my keeper."

Karen flinched as if she had been struck. Then, suddenly, she knew they had got past the place where Christopher could be rude and where it did not matter because she could make excuses for him. There was no possible excuse for deliberate unkindness like this, and if there was any hope at all for them as husband and wife then Christopher must understand that.

"You do not have to tell me that, Christopher," she said quietly. "I have understood for a long time just why you married me."

She went out of the room, shutting the door gently behind her and the three people left behind were silent. Christopher because he was furious with her for showing himself in far from flattering colours, and even more with himself for having put himself into a position where such a thing was possible. Stella was frankly startled at the girl's astuteness and Fred was completely bewildered.

Suddenly Christopher said:

"Ring for Bannister, please."

The man came in and Christopher gave a curt order for him to be wheeled back to his own room.

Stella shrugged her shoulders as the door closed behind him, but Fred gave voice to his perplexities.

"Now, what was all that about?" he asked her. "Could you pick it up?"

"Pick what up?" Stella fenced.

"What Karen said about knowing why Kit married her," he puzzled. "It sounded almost as if—well, as if he didn't care for her and she knew it."

"Did it?" Stella contrived to keep a sardonic note out of her voice. "Oh—do you think that is likely?"

"No; I shouldn't think Karen was the sort of girl that

126

would marry for anything but love," he said stoutly. "All the same, she was badly upset." He stood frowning for a moment; then, with an impatient gesture, he flung his cigarette into the fire. "Oh, damn it. I hate things being— uncomfortable," he said explosively. "If I were clever so that I knew what to do—but I don't." He sighed, and Stella looked at him curiously.

"Would you like us to go home?" she suggested. "After all, Kit can't expect us always to put his interests before our own."

Fred took her hand in his and lifted it gently to his lips.

"There's nothing I'd sooner do," he assured her wistfully. "But—somehow or other, I can't bring myself to telling the old chap so. Oh I know he's difficult and queer at times, but he and I have always been something more than cousins. We've been real friends—and I want to stand by him a bit longer, anyway. Do you understand?"

"Of course," she said sweetly. Really, it was too absurd! Fred had been on the point of feeling that he could not stand being at Claverings any more and it had only needed just the slightest suggestion on her part that they should leave to make him take the opposite point of view. Really it was boringly simple to twist Fred round her little finger— without him ever knowing it!

Karen pressed her hot face against the cool pane of her bedroom window. Outside, the night was bright with clear, cold starlight and there was an answering chill in her heart.

It was no good refusing to face up to it. Christopher's anger had not been for the superficial reason which he had given. That was only a surface reaction. The real trouble went far deeper than that.

In spite of his remark that in a way it had been easier when he had believed that he had only a short time to live, none the less, she knew that a new hope for his recovery had been born in him. It showed in his willingness to co-operate in the treatment that he was having. And at first that new hope must have been all-sufficient. But now he had become more accustomed to the idea, he must have begun to realise something else. It was one thing to have married a girl he did not even know when he expected to be dead in a few months. A very different situation now that he might live, saddled with an unwanted wife.

And all the more unwanted, Karen thought sadly, because her presence was a constant reminder to him of that self which he probably loathed now. For it was obvious that either he had forgiven Stella or even believed that there was nothing to forgive. Stella had been very clever. She had never tried to defend herself—and that was the surest way of convincing people that there was nothing requiring defence.

But Stella was not the sort lightly to relinquish her claim on anything which she regarded as her own. Not for a moment did Karen credit Stella with really loving Christopher or being any more anxious now than she ever had been to shoulder the burden of an invalid husband. But for the sake of her own self-esteem, she would be quite callous in tormenting Christopher with her desirability. And, in a way, it did not matter what Stella's feelings were. To Karen, hating strife and longing for Christopher's love, life would be intolerable shared with him in such circumstances. But—Christopher might not get better. All his hopes might be shattered and then Stella would certainly lose all interest in him. And Christopher, needing comfort and reassurance, might turn to her as he had done once before in his hour of need. Yes; that was the one thing that really mattered. No matter how much he hurt her or how much Stella indulged in those hateful little pin-pricks at which she was so clever, she would—must—stick it out until they knew for sure what was going to happen.

And even if he got better, surely there was just a chance of them building some sort of life together—oh, not the heart-tearing sweetness of a love match but at least something that was fine and good. Yes; it was possible. If he did not find that, in spite of everything, he still loved Stella——

And then, abruptly, she ceased to dream of the possible future and thought, instead, of the past—the immediate past.

Herself, just now, asking Christopher to remember Dr. Stalham's warning. Christopher flushing and moving his hand impatiently—which hand? His right one or the one that he had never been able to move since his accident? She pressed her fingers against her temples as she tried to recall the relative positions of herself and Christopher. She had been standing between him and the fireplace and he had moved the hand nearer to her. The *left* hand!

"Oh——" Her breath passed her lips in a long, fluttering sigh. Then, groping blindly, she flung herself beside the window seat and wept in gratitude for what this could mean for Christopher—and perhaps just a little bit for her own troubled heart.

Both the Pilbrights and Aunt Sarah accepted the invitations that were issued to them, and Aunt Sarah arrived early, ostensibly in order to help, but actually because she dearly loved to know all that was going on at first hand. However, she was too energetic to remain idle, and she helped decorate the big ballroom where the children's party was to be and personally dug up the Christmas tree that was to be brought indoors and decorated.

Stella, completely bored with her trip to Town for the gifts that were to go on it, willingly relinquished all pretence at sorting them out and putting the name tags on them. Aunt Sarah sniffed disparagingly at her choice.

"Oh, nice enough, no doubt," she said critically. "But what is Mrs. Pooker going to say if her Dorlena has a cheaper present than Mrs. Diffey's Carol? They ought all to have cost as near the same as possible, and they obviously haven't. Oh, well, I suppose there's nothing can be done about it!"

"I wonder," Karen said thoughtfully. "Look, Miss Sarah, if instead of putting a name on each parcel we put a number—in red for boys and green for girls. Then each child must draw a number from a hat and get the corresponding parcel off the tree—would that do?"

"It's an inspiration!" Miss Sarah said emphatically. "And, for goodness' sake, child, call me Aunt. After all, you are my nephew's wife, you know, though sometimes I wonder if you quite realise it!"

Karen turned away, ostensibly to gather up some of the wrapping paper that lay about.

"Not always," she admitted. "But then—it isn't quite an

ordinary sort of marriage like most others, you know."

"So I realise," the old lady admitted, looking at her with not unkind curiosity. "As a matter of fact, I would very much like to know the true story of it all, but I don't suppose for a minute you will tell me, so don't begin to think up excuses! I admire people who know when to hold their tongues, even if I don't myself!"

Karen came and laid her hand on Miss Sarah's wrinkled one.

"I think—if anyone took you into their confidence you would be very loyal and not breathe a word about it," she said earnestly. "But—there are some things that are better not discussed, particularly when they concern more than one person."

"You are quite right, child," Miss Sarah agreed; and then, briskly: "Well, this won't do! We must get on."

They worked steadily, and in a far shorter time than Karen had believed possible they were ready for Fred to come and hang the things on the tree.

Each gift was wrapped in bright-coloured paper and each parcel carried its number. In addition, there were bags of sweets and tinsel and glass decorations. On the top, a big shining star.

Karen regarded it with wide, childlike eyes and Fred, suddenly aware of the wistful droop of her lips, slipped his hand under her arm.

"Is this the first one you've ever seen?" he asked gently, and she nodded.

"Nobody ever bothered in houses I've been, even though some of them had children of their own," she said, her eyes on the sparkling star. "Christmas wasn't anything special—and it ought to be! Oh, Fred, it ought to be! Particularly when there are children. If I had my way, every child should remember Christmas as the most wonderful day of their lives!"

Above her head, Fred met Miss Sarah's eyes, which she was frankly mopping. His own felt suspiciously like watering.

"Never mind, old lady," he said consolingly. "You're being fairy godmother and giving all these kids something to remember; so that's something, isn't it?"

"Yes, of course it is," she admitted and smiled.

"That's better," Fred said encouragingly. "And now for the mistletoe!"

He hung a big bunch on each of the crystal chandeliers and inspected it critically.

"I hope it works all right!" he murmured and with an all encompassing sweep of his long arms caught hold of both Karen and Miss Sarah. "Now then, one each!" he insisted and kissed them both heartily.

Miss Sarah took it as her just due, but Karen broke away laughing and blushing, and shortly after, she made some excuse to run away.

"H'm. Now, I wonder, is Christopher too big a fool to realise what a very lovely girl he has married?" Miss Sarah mused.

"She *is* lovely," Fred agreed. "But—there is still so much of the child in her, I wonder—I mean, I never think of her as being grown up, a woman."

"Desirable, you mean," Miss Sarah said bluntly. "No; but then you've never looked in any save one direction, have you, Fred?"

"No," he admitted simply. "It's always been Stella as far as I am concerned. And it will always be—no matter what happens."

"And I wonder just what that means," Miss Sarah asked herself. "And if he quite knows himself."

The Pilbrights came down on Christmas Eve and Karen went to the station herself to meet them. Miss Pilbright greeted Karen warmly and then, holding her at arm's length, said critically:

"You're thinner! What have you been doing to yourself?"

Karen laughed and shrugged her shoulders.

"Nothing. I expect that's the trouble. I'm used to being very busy and I expect I thrive on that more than on being a lady of leisure!"

"H'm," said Miss Pilbright doubtfully and stood aside for her brother to tender his greetings.

He made no comment about Karen's appearance but later he told his sister that she was quite right. She was thinner—and she was not happy.

"I feel most concerned," he told her earnestly. "After all, I was largely responsible."

"It's too late to worry about that," she pointed out philosophically. "And, after all, if Karen had not married Mr. Thirlby, who knows, she might have been still unhappier. No, the thing to do is find out what is wrong and try to put it right!"

But superficially there was nothing wrong at all. Since that outburst, Christopher had treated Karen with scrupulous politeness. It was true that his very politeness held her at arm's length but there was little difference, after all, between that and the way in which any man, not given to demonstrativeness in public, would treat his wife before guests.

Mr. Pilbright cheered up quite considerably, and if Miss Pilbright's shrewder, woman's eyes saw deeper, she said nothing to disturb him.

Actually, she and Miss Sarah spent a lot of time together and appeared to have plenty to talk about.

It had not taken either Miss Pilbright or Miss Sarah long to discover that they shared a common interest and liking for Karen. And by the time Christmas Day was half over, both were in possession of an almost complete comprehension of the two Thirlby marriages and what had led up to them.

"If my brother had realised what lay behind it all," Miss Pilbright said worriedly, "I am sure that he would have refused point-blank to have anything to do with the matter."

"H'm," deliberated Miss Sarah. "Probably. But it is not a bad thing, after all. For one thing, each has something to forgive the other."

"I don't see that," Miss Pilbright objected stoutly. "If, as you say, Christopher Thirlby married a nice little girl like that simply to score off a girl who had the sense to jilt him, then certainly Karen has something to forgive. But I don't see that she has done anything which he can logically resent."

"What other motive could she have had than the security which his money has given her?" Miss Sarah insisted. "Oh, I admit, she has more than done her duty by him, but the fact remains, none the less."

"M'm," mused Miss Pilbright. "That is something that I have often wondered about. It seems so out of character and yet—she could not have fallen in love with him, could she? I mean, there was not time."

"Oh, if it comes to that," Miss Sarah admitted, "one can fall in love in no time at all! And, after all, pity is akin to love—it could be."

Miss Pilbright hesitated.

"I think I hope that it isn't," she confessed. "Because if it is, I am afraid that Karen is going to be very unhappy—whatever happens to Christopher in the future."

"I shall do my best to see that events prove you to be wrong," Miss Sarah stated firmly.

"So shall I—if opportunity offers itself," Miss Pilbright agreed. And sighed. "But you know how it is with these young people. They are disinclined to take advice—least of all from an unmarried woman of uncertain age."

"There's no uncertainty about *my* age," Miss Sarah said spiritedly. "I am seventy-six and I don't mind who knows it."

"Probably I shan't either when I reach that age," Miss Pilbright said sweetly, and took out her knitting.

Karen had selected the reddish-brown dress, of which Madame Zelia had been particularly proud, to wear at the party. It was cheerful and cosy besides, which was as well, because, though the ballroom was heated, its very size kept it from being really warm. She was wearing Christopher's Christmas present, twin bracelets that clasped over the close-fitting wrist of each sleeve. There was something a little barbaric about them, a tawny tint to the gold, perhaps, or something in their design; and yet, strangely, they looked just right on Karen. They were, she realised, very lovely, and she had thanked Christopher for them very sincerely, yet, because she knew quite well that only convention and not the desire to make her a gift had caused him to buy them for her, there had been little or no spontaneous pleasure in her voice. Christopher had made no comment, but his lips twisted sardonically as, in turn, he gravely thanked her for her gift.

It had not been easy to decide what to give him. In the

end she had fallen back on what she felt were far from imaginative gifts—books and gramophone records.

"Just what I wanted!" he declared and Karen winced because she knew that he had realised her difficulty—there were so few things now that were of any use to him.

She was thinking of this now as she stood waiting in the ballroom for the first of the guests. Fred was tacking up a few festoons that had come unfastened and Miss Sarah was surreptitiously sampling sandwiches already laid out. Christopher was to come in just for a little while, when the gifts were presented.

Her not very happy thoughts were interrupted by Stella's entry, and both girls looked a little startled. For Stella, too, was wearing a red frock. It was a brighter colour than Karen's and her white arms were bare, but none the less it emphasised the likeness between them.

"Heavenly twins!" she commented sardonically. "Really, Karen, we shall have to do something about this! Will you change or shall I?"

But before they could do any such thing, the children were arriving and, after that, no grown-up had any time to think of their own affairs.

It was a noisy, happy party and everything that had been done appeared to meet with their approval. And, as Miss Sarah said, why not? They had far too much to eat, made a lot too much noise, and for once in a way had escaped from maternal vigilance.

"And few children ask more than that," she insisted.

Even Christopher's appearance did not sober them, for they simply took it for granted that it was just one more oddness of which grown-ups were capable, in that he should address them from a couch instead of standing up. And Christopher, with a courage that made Karen's eyes prick with unshed tears, spoke to them gaily and amusingly, as if he, like them, had had all his wishes gratified.

Then, rather to everyone's relief, for the smaller children were beginning to get tearful with all the excitement, it was time for them to go. Fred stayed in the suddenly quiet ballroom to make sure that all the fairy lights were safely disconnected and Karen, though tired, went to thank Mrs. Paynton and Cook for their share in the party.

Stella went downstairs wondering how it was possible that everybody did not feel as bored as she did. It was odd, she thought, that Kit had this almost old-fashioned determination to do what he thought was his duty by his tenants. But then, she had to admit, Kit was rather an enigma at times. You could never tell which self would be uppermost.

She found Christopher already in the lounge. He was dozing, and with a shrug she knelt down by the fire. It was very peaceful—or boring, if you saw it that way. And then, so quickly that she could not get out of the way, a live coal suddenly shot out of the fire right into her lap.

All her poise and sophistication vanished. As the flames flickered over her dress sheer panic gripped her and she screamed:

"Kit, Kit! Do something!"

And Christopher, startled to wakefulness by her screams, Christopher who had been helpless for months, threw back his coverlet and, with an answering cry, staggered across the room to her aid.

CHAPTER NINE

STELLA'S screams brought the others running into the room, but before they got there Christopher had already beaten out the flames. He was now sitting in a big armchair, his eyes covered with his hand while Stella, still sobbing hysterically, was staring down at the ruin of her dress with wide, frightened eyes.

But neither Karen nor even Fred had any eyes for her. As she came into the room, Karen caught her breath and, without stopping to think of anything save this miracle, ran to Christopher and dropped on her knees beside him.

"Christopher, darling!" she said unsteadily. "What happened?"

He put an arm round her shaking shoulders and again she had that blissful feeling that he was depending on her.

"I—don't—quite—know," he said slowly. "I heard a scream—I was half asleep, I think. And—the next thing I knew I was kneeling on the floor beating the flames out of—Stella's dress."

Gently Karen turned his hands over. They were less badly hurt than she had feared, but they needed attention, and over her shoulder she told Bannister, who had come hurrying in behind them, to get some dressing for them.

"But first, ring up Dr. Stalham," she told him. Then she turned back to Christopher. "Is it all right to sit up until Dr. Stalham comes, do you think? Or ought you to lie down again?"

"To tell you the truth, I don't think I can get up again—yet," he confessed. "I feel as boneless as a jelly-fish."

"Yes; I expect you do," Karen said gently, but continued firmly and reassuringly: "One always does after spending some time in bed. It will probably take quite a long time for you to get really strong just because of that."

"Karen, shall I get better?" he whispered like a frightened child. Her hand closed reassuringly over his wrist.

"Yes," she said with utter conviction. "You've had a miracle worked especially for you, Christopher. There is nothing to be afraid of."

He leaned back in the chair with a little sigh.

"I'm almost afraid to believe it and yet—I think you are right," he admitted.

Bannister came in with the dressings and, in addition, a small glass with a dark pinkish fluid in it.

"I think this will do her ladyship good, sir," he said, handing it to Fred. "Only sal volatile with a few other stimulants added."

Fred put his arms round Stella and held the glass to her lips. She drank mechanically as if she hardly realised what she was doing, and his kind face grew anxious. He waited until she had finished the medicine and then, in a way that precluded any protests she might have made, he said.

"I'm going to take you up to bed. You've had a shock, and that is the best place for you. Bannister, I wonder if you could get hold of her ladyship's maid?" And then, as easily and confidently as if she had been a child, he picked her up and carried her out of the room.

Unconsciously, Karen gave a little sigh of relief.

"I can finish bandaging, Bannister," she suggested. "And then you can see about sending Flora up. Tell her to take hot-water bottles, and have a cup of tea sent as well."

"You think of everything, don't you?" Christopher said, looking at the top of her bent head as she knelt in front of him securing the end of the bandage.

She looked up at him fleetingly, her cheeks stained with sudden colour.

"No, not always," she said with a little sigh. "Sometimes I make silly mistakes. Not because I don't try not to, but because I can't always see other people's points of view." She sat back on her heels and looked at him gravely. She felt nearer to him than she had ever done before and she found the courage to say things that, a short hour before, would have been impossible. "Christopher, I only went out riding with Fred because the doctor said I had got to get out and have some exercise. It wasn't because I—because I particularly wanted to. As a matter of fact, I was dreadfully frightened!"

137

"Were you?" He seemed amused at that. Then his expression changed. "But you kept on going out," he reminded her.

"I had to get unafraid," she said seriously. "I thought—when you got better—it would be nice if we could ride together."

He looked at her in amazement.

"What made you so sure?" he asked. "I've had practically no hope at all."

"Oh," she said thoughtfully, "I hoped so much—I tried to *believe* you into getting well."

"And it looks as if you succeeded in doing it." He surveyed her wonderingly. "Karen——"

He leaned towards her, but at that moment her quick ears caught a little sound.

"The doctor!" she said, scrambling hastily to her feet. "Would you like to see him alone, Christopher? Or shall I stay?"

"Stay," he said, lying back in the chair again and smiling up at her. "Do you know, Mrs. Thirlby, you are rather a wonderful young person?"

The quick colour surged again into her pale cheeks and for a moment her hand lay lightly on his shoulder.

"And you've forgiven me?" she asked softly.

"At the moment, I feel as if I could forgive anybody anything," he said reflectively, and then Dr. Stalham came in.

He listened in silence while Christopher told him what had happened, and then he nodded.

"Yes; I fancy it was something along those lines that Braunton expected. Oh, not Lady Thirlby's dress catching fire, but something that would provide an impetus. Of course, you realise that now, of all times, you can't play the fool. You must make haste slowly. Of course, we must have Braunton down. In fact, I think I'll try to get him on the 'phone now. And in the meantime—I don't want to be a spoil sport, but I think you had better get flat again. Oh yes; it won't do you any harm to walk over to your bed!"

It was an appreciable effort now for Christopher to get up, but he managed it unaided and walked slowly across the room with a most wonderful feeling of exhilaration.

"You don't think it was just a flash in the pan, do you?" he asked anxiously. "I mean—I just didn't stop to think before—it just happened as if I had been completely well. Whereas this time——"

"What you forget is that in such circumstances you naturally thought of nothing but Lady Thirlby's need," Dr. Stalham said cheerfully. "Now you've had time to think about yourself again. Besides that, seeing anybody in flames is a shock in itself. I've seen it once and I remember feeling a complete wreck for hours later."

"Something in that," Christopher agreed.

Fortunately, Forster Braunton was in, and immediately he heard what had happened he insisted on coming down then and there.

"I shall have to beg for a bed," he said. "And also I shall have to make a very early start back to Town, but this is too miraculous for any chances to be taken!"

Dr. Stalham accepted the responsibility of telling him that that would be quite all right and then went back to report the news.

"If I were you, I'd turn in for the night now," he told Christopher, after Karen had gone off to make arrangements for Mr. Braunton's room. He spoke a little doubtfully, as if he were not quite sure whether Christopher would do as he suggested, and Christopher laughed.

"You needn't worry, Doctor. I shall be an entirely tractable patient now! After all, I've surely sufficient incentive to be!"

"Yes; you have," Dr. Stalham said thoughtfully, his eyes on the door through which Karen had vanished. "Well, I'd better get hold of Bannister to lend you a hand and then I'll go and see Lady Thirlby. Do you think she was much hurt?"

"Not at all, I fancy," Christopher said with evident relief. "But, of course, it was a shock."

"Quite," the doctor agreed drily. He had no particular affection for Stella, whom he considered both hard and selfish.

He met Fred on the stairs—a rather worried, unhappy Fred whose face lightened when he saw the doctor.

"I was just coming down to ask you to see Stella," he said. "She's—in a very queer state. She doesn't seem to see anything. It's as if she's got a picture before her eyes of something she's thinking about. I suppose it's reaction from the shock."

"Now, don't you get trying to take my job away," Dr. Stalham said pleasantly. "I'll do the diagnosing, if you don't mind! Coming up?"

"No; I don't think so," Fred said hesitatingly. "You see, I rather worried her, pottering about in the room. I'm one of those big, clumsy blighters, you know," he added with a rather twisted smile. "Enough to get on any woman's nerves! You go on up. It's Kit's old room, along the main corridor. Her maid is with her."

Dr. Stalham found Stella propped up in bed and, in spite of his reproof to Fred, he had to admit that his own diagnosis was exactly the same. He came to the side of the bed and Stella appeared to be unaware of his presence. In a rather sharp voice he spoke her name.

"Lady Thirlby!"

She started a little at that and looked towards him. To his relief, there was none of the blank, fearful expression that he had half anticipated. Instead, something that puzzled him. He could have sworn that not only was she in very full possession of her faculties, but that the thoughts which had absorbed her were entirely pleasant. Quite evidently, Lady Thirlby had got over the shock of what had happened. In that case, though, it seemed odd that she had sent poor old Fred away.

She put out her hand eagerly.

"Will Kit get really better?"

The doctor hesitated. Downstairs, he had told the two people most nearly concerned that he felt little doubt as to Christopher's complete recovery. Now he felt a strong inclination to suggest that there was more than a little doubt about it. Not because he really felt that there was, but because it seemed just rather too important to Lady Thirlby that he should get better. Then he told himself that he was being imaginative, that it was natural enough that she should be anxious. And, in any case, she would soon know the truth.

"I believe he will. Braunton is coming down to see him this evening. Then we shall know for sure. Or, at least, as sure as one humanly can be."

She nodded slowly.

"It's incredible," she said almost under her breath. "How could one possibly have guessed." She stopped abruptly and looked at him sharply as she realised that his grave eyes were fixed inquiringly on her. She relaxed against her pillows and said, in a faint voice: "I wish you'd give me a sedative, Doctor. I have a feeling that I shan't sleep a wink all night if you don't."

He nodded in agreement.

It was a reasonable enough request and before he went slowly and thoughtfully downstairs he left a couple of tablets for her to take.

An hour or so later the surgeon arrived. He was obviously in high spirits at the news and clapped Dr. Stalham on the shoulder.

"How does he seem?" he asked as he took off his coat and gloves.

"A bit dazed," Dr. Stalham said judicially. "But I think he'll be all right. A little bit inclined to worry whether it's permanent or not. I assured him that there was little danger of a relapse, providing he is sensible."

"H'm." Braunton hesitated. "I hope you're right. He doesn't seem the type one can rely on to take orders—these beggars who are used to giving them rarely are. However, we'd better go in to him."

Half an hour later, Braunton gave his opinion.

"Yes, you ought to be all right now," he admitted. "But I want to make sure."

"How?" Christopher asked tersely.

"Put yourself complètely in my hands for a month," Forster Braunton told him.

"Just exactly what does than mean?"

The surgeon sat down on the edge of the bed, his hands linked round one knee.

"I want you under my own eye for that time," he explained. "I want to see that you have regular exercise and that you don't overdo it."

"You don't trust me, then?"

"Do you trust yourself?" the other man asked curiously.

"No; I suppose I don't," he admitted. "All right, a month, then. When?"

Braunton hesitated.

"In a day or two," he said at last. "I'd say at once, but I'd sooner you didn't have to take a journey until you've got over this excitement. Spend the time quietly with your wife."

"Karen." Christopher's dark brows met quickly. "No, it wouldn't be fair. Look here, Braunton, unless you think it would be really dangerous, I would sooner go away to-morrow. And—I wonder if you would do something for me?"

"Of course, if I can."

"I want you to tell my wife—I think it would be better," Christopher said slowly. "I want you to make the necessity of it very clear to her. Do you understand?"

Forster Braunton nodded. It was a reasonable enough explanation and yet he felt that something more lay behind the intensity with which his patient spoke.

"I'll go and tell her now," he said, getting up.

He found Karen in the hall and in a few brief sentences explained the situation.

"Your husband is very anxious that you should understand how much importance I attach to this," he said precisely. "I imagine he is afraid that it will upset you that he should go away. And, of course, I quite appreciate the fact that at such a moment you would prefer to be together. None the less, you will be doing him a great service, Mrs. Thirlby, if you will assure him of your complete understanding and agreement with him doing this. Do you understand?"

"You mean, if I were to make a fuss it might worry him and make it harder to give all his mind to getting better?" she said eagerly. "Yes, of course I understand, Mr. Braunton, and I will do exactly what you suggest."

"That's good," he said approvingly. "Just take it as a matter of course. And now, about actual arrangements."

A brisk working out of suitable times, a couple of telephone calls, and it was all settled. Christopher would leave Claverings the following morning for the nursing-home which Mr. Braunton recommended. Then Fred took the surgeon off to have a drink and Karen went to tell Christopher what they had arranged. She found Stella with him and, as she came in, Stella stopped speaking, so that it made her feel as if she had interrupted a confidential chat.

"Well?" Christopher said eagerly.

"Mr. Braunton has arranged everything," Karen answered with a serenity that she was far from feeling. "The ambulance will come at eleven. Have you told Bannister what you want packed?"

"Not yet." He paused. "Good Lord! I suppose I shall have to take ordinary day clothes!"

She knew that he was marvelling at the wonderful thing that had happened, but since, for Christopher's sake, there must be no emotional scenes, no fussing, she seized on his remark and treated it with practical common sense.

"Yes, of course. And sports things—something you could wear in a gymnasium." She bit her lip as there surged into her mind the realisation of just what this meant. Christopher fit and well. But that was in the future. For a whole month he would be away from Claverings and she, presumably, would have to stay there all alone. It would seem horribly big and empty. "I think I'll go and have a word with Bannister," she said and hurried out of the room.

Stella looked after her thoughtfully.

"How odd," she said reflectively.

"What?" Christopher asked shortly.

She gave a little start.

"Oh—I'm sorry, Kit, I didn't realise that I was speaking aloud!"

"Well, you were," he said deliberately. "So you may as well finish saying what was in your mind!"

"Oh—nothing!" she hedged.

"I think it was something quite definite," he insisted. "Tell me!"

"Oh—really, Kit!" she protested. "It was only—just a passing thought that—Karen is in a frightful hurry to get you off! Almost as if she were glad——" Her voice trailed to silence and out of the corner of her eye she saw the irritation she had aroused.

"It was I who insisted on getting off at once," he told her. "Braunton suggested waiting a few days, but I prefer to go now. And as for Karen being glad, why shouldn't she be? Aren't you glad that this has happened? Wouldn't any decently good-natured person be glad for my sake?"

"Oh, Kit, of course!" she said reproachfully. "You know I didn't mean that! I do wish you hadn't made me say anything because—thoughts become so much more concrete when one puts them into words. Please do forget what I said!"

But she knew perfectly well that he would not forget. For Kit, these days, was a different person from the man she had known for many years. Something besides his accident had happened to him. Or could happen at any time now. For she did not think that he realised the change in himself or what it meant. Nor, she was sure, did Karen.

The truth was that he was on the verge of imagining himself in love with that colourless, insignificant little interloper. That was why he had been so angry with Karen for going out riding with Fred. He was jealous and, even allowing for the mental effect that his helpless condition must have had, incredibly lacking in self-confidence. Kit, who had always been so sure of himself, suddenly humble and unsure on account of a girl that he had bribed to marry him!

It was incredible—and intolerable! Humiliating to Stella to know that her picture had been blotted out of his mind because that of another girl had taken her place! And she had no doubts but that she was perfectly right. He was completely indifferent to her now—so indifferent that he could be quite pleasant to her—as one would be to a new acquaintance who was also a guest. No; she just didn't matter to him any more except as his cousin's wife. Stella's even teeth grated against each other. Kit's money now entered far less into her calculations than the need which her vanity had to see him again a suppliant for her favours. For she was shrewd enough to see that, in spite of the barriers which their incredible marriage had erected, Kit and Karen were on the brink of realising that they loved one another. And once that had happened——

Inexorably the minutes and hours crept by. To Karen's ears, every clock in the house was a malevolent being deliberately shortening the time that she and Christopher had together before the ambulance came.

For, to her, there was something final in this parting—unless Christopher said something that would make a bridge from the life that they had so far spent together to the new life that would start when Christopher left the nursing-home. Would they share it? Would there be a place in his plans for her? She busied herself with little jobs—always keeping within call of Christopher, and at last he seemed to arouse himself from the lethargy which had held him in its grip all the morning and spoke her name.

She came to him quickly and stood beside him.

"I'm afraid I haven't been very sociable this morning," he said, not so much apologetically as if he were compelled to say it. "It's queer but this new development seems far less real and convincing than when they told me I was completely finished. It's as if I am dreaming it and unless I keep very quiet and still, I shall wake up and find it *is* all a dream."

"I know," she nodded, and it was true. It was how she had felt for a long time—one day, if she was not careful, she would wake up and find that, after all, she was not Christopher's wife.

"Do you?" he pondered. "Yes; I expect you do. Probably we all find it easier to believe the unpleasant things of life than the pleasant ones—although, to be quite honest, I never stopped to think about such things before my crash."

"Christopher, there's something——" she began hesitatingly.

"Yes?" he said sharply, his dark eyes intent on her face.

"When you are better, are you going to fly again?" she asked timidly.

He thought for a moment, then he shook his head.

"No." There was regret in his tone, but he sounded quite positive. "At least, I shall probably fly—be flown, rather—if it is convenient. After all, it's as safe as travelling by train or boat. But—test-flying, no; I've finished that. Somehow or other, it's lost its appeal. I suppose some people would say it was cowardice, but——"

"Oh no!" she said indignantly.

He shrugged his shoulders ever so slightly.

"Well, I couldn't give any other good reason," he admitted. There was a little pause and then he said again: "Karen?"

"Yes, Christopher?" she said eagerly.

"While I'm away, what are you going to do?"

"I haven't thought," she confessed. "It's all happened so suddenly."

"That's true," he agreed. "Well, what would you like to do?"

She shook her head. Impossible to tell him that the one thing that she wanted to do was to come wih him.

"Well, if you haven't any definite plans, will you do what I'd like you to?" he asked.

"Oh—yes, of course," she said eagerly. "Anything."

"Look, my dear. You've seen very little of the world—either geographically or, shall we say, socially. I mean, you haven't met many people, have you?"

"No," she admitted. "I haven't. But I think I am more the sort of person that likes a small circle of friends who really like me than lots and lots of people who hardly know me at all."

"Probably you are," he said thoughtfully. "All the same, Karen, I've made up my mind to arrange with Pilbright that you are to have a definite income settled on you."

"Oh—Christopher—no," she protested.

"Don't be a silly little idiot," he said impatiently. "Don't you see, I am trying to do the best for both of us?"

Her eyes flickered momentarily.

"Very well, Christopher," she said docilely.

"That's a good child," he said lightly. "Well, all it amounts to is this. While I am in the nursing-home, I want you to have a real holiday. Forget all about me for a little while and give yourself a chance of blossoming out a bit. Meet people, travel. Oh, I know it will all be unfamiliar to you and you'd probably rather stay in your own little nook, but——"

"It's a good plan," she reassured him gently, "I quite understand and I will do exactly what you think is best."

"Good!" he said with evident relief. "Then—don't come

and see me and don't write, and, that way, when we meet again it will be as completely new people from the ones that we have been up to now. That should give us the best chance——" He spoke the last words under his breath and Karen was quick to realise their significance.

For she realised that what Christopher was saying was that though what she was when he had thought he was dying had not mattered, it was different now. How could he help knowing that she was neither sufficiently well educated nor experienced in the ways of the world to which he belonged to be able to take her place before the world as his wife when he was a whole man again?

And humbly she admitted that it was true. And just as he had been given a chance, so, now, he was giving her one. And, for the moment, she did not stop to consider whether it was love or justice that had prompted him. It hardly mattered. It was what Christopher wanted her to do and that was enough.

"Shall I come with you in the ambulance?" she asked timidly.

"No," he said shortly. "Better not." He raised himself slightly. "Listen! Is that the ambulance?"

She glanced at her watch. "I expect so," she said, forcing herself to be calm. She bent over him, lightly touching his hand. "Christopher, get better!" she said earnestly. "Whatever else happens, that's the most important thing."

He caught her hand.

"Karen——" he began sharply and then Bannister came in.

"The ambulance has arrived, sir."

And the moment that, to Karen, had suddenly seemed fraught with desperate importance passed. In an incredibly short time, Christopher had gone and she was left behind.

Even Stella was surprisesd that Karen did not go with Christopher, but she made no comment, and it was Miss Sarah who put the question that was in everybody's mind.

"What are you going to do, Karen?"

"Do?" she said thoughtfully. "Oh—Christopher and I planned that. I shall stay here for a little while and then—I shall try to find someone who will—coach me to—to—

well, to be the sort of person that Christopher's wife ought to be."

They stared at her in amazement, and Karen flushed.

"It is a very sensible idea," she said gravely. "You see, I have never had the advantages that most people have as a matter of course and——"

"But, my dear girl, you can't learn things like that as if they were school lessons!" Stella said impatiently. "You have to grow up knowing."

"Or else you just have to have an instinct for them, as Karen has," Miss Sarah interposed very quietly. "As Christopher ought to have realised for himself. None the less, I think it is a good idea. If ever a girl has earned a holiday, Karen has and I shall see to it that she has a good one! I have plenty of friends who will welcome her, first for my sake, and then, I am sure, for her own. We will have a talk about it later, Karen, shall we?"

"Please, Aunt Sarah," Karen said gratefully.

"But, I say," Fred began disapprovingly. "*We* ought to be the people that trot Karen about, if that's what she wants to do. I mean, after all, you'd rather be with us than strangers, wouldn't you, Karen?"

She hesitated and Stella cut in:

"Darling, a couple of old marrieds, like us, won't be much fun for Karen! Don't embarrass her by trying to make over her arrangements for her!"

"It's very dear of you," Karen said gently, seeing the hurt look in Fred's eyes. "But you must want to get back to your own home. And, after all, you will still be looking after things here for Christopher, though I know he feels it is asking an awful lot of you."

The subject dropped after that. After lunch, Mr. Pilbright and his sister started back to Town and Miss Sarah asked Fred if he would run her back to her cottage.

"Karen must be tired out with all this business," she insisted. "And the fewer visitors she has the better. But come and see me as soon as you are ready to, child."

"I will," Karen said gratefully.

"You two girls will be all right on your own, won't you?" Fred asked. Stella nodded.

"Absolutely," she said sweetly. "Karen and I have not

had many chances of getting to know one another properly. This will be quite a good one!"

Fred looked at her with that half-troubled, half-puzzled expression that Stella's remarks so often brought to his kindly face. Then he squared his shoulders as if he were trying to throw off a burden and went off on his job.

For a moment there was silence, then Stella said slowly: "Really, there are times when one would almost think that Fred was amazingly tactful—if one didn't know that such a thing were impossible! I expect you realise, as I do, that it certainly is time that we had a talk!"

But Karen hardly heard her last sentence. Her face was too expressive to be able to hide the distaste which Stella's remark aroused in her, and Stella, seeing it, laughed.

"Now what have I done?" she asked.

"I—wish—why do you say such beastly things about Fred?" she asked unhappily. "He's so nice."

Stella yawned.

"My dear girl, he's *too* nice—if that is the right word! And he bores me to distraction! Still, that doesn't matter much—yet. What I want to talk about is you and Kit."

Still Karen did not speak and Stella went on deliberately:

"Your marriage has got to be wiped out, you know."

"No!" Karen said sharply, sitting very erect.

Stella laughed softly.

"You little fool, you'll never keep him now he is well," she jibed, noting with satisfaction the way in which Karen flinched. "Oh, I admit that you are an excellent nurse and that he has come to rely on you to quite an amazing extent. You've been extraordinarily clever—far more clever than I thought you were capable of being."

"It wasn't cleverness," Karen said briefly.

"No? Well, it hardly matters. What does matter is that once Kit is better, he won't need a nurse. He will need—the woman that he loves."

"You?" Karen said disdainfully. "After you jilted him to marry Fred because of Christopher's accident. I don't think that is likely to happen!"

"But then, my pet, you know so little about men!" Stella stared down at her engagement ring and twiddled it gently, a faint but confident smile curving her lips. "Oh, I know Kit hated me! There is only a very thin line, you know, between love and hatred!"

"And you think he has crossed that line again and that he loves you now?" Karen said defiantly. "I don't believe it!"

Stella's eyes narrowed.

"All these weeks you've been trying to get Kit to move, haven't you? And he's not so much as crooked his little finger!"

"He has!" Karen said triumphantly. "That first night he spent in the lounge!"

"So he did. I forgot," Stella said mockingly. "He was so annoyed with you that he lifted his hand to motion you away, didn't he?"

Karen stood up.

"Stella, this is—horrible," she said, speaking with difficulty. "If there is anything you think it is important to say, please say it and get it over, because I can't stand much more."

Stella tilted her head back against the bright silk cushion and looked calculatingly up at the pale girl whose nerves were obviously strained to breaking-point.

"All right," she said carelessly. "There isn't much I want to say. Just this—Mr. Braunton wanted Christopher to wait a few days before he went away. But Christopher insisted on going at once. Need I point out why?"

"Go on," Karen said stonily.

Stella shrugged.

"Very well. Have you realised that it was for me—to save *me* that Kit made the effort to get up? You had not been able to get him to do that. Nobody had. But for my sake—because he loves me——"

She stopped. There was no need to go on. Karen's dazed, stricken face told her that.

CHAPTER TEN

KAREN's dry lips parted.

"No!" she whispered. "No—— He can't love *you!*"

A thinner-skinned person than Stella might have flinched at the contempt in Karen's voice, but she only shrugged her shoulders.

"My dear girl, most people would say that you cannot possibly love Kit after the way in which he has treated you, but you seem to find no difficulty in doing it!" she pointed out pertinently.

That was perfectly true, and Karen could find no answer to it.

"But—but he was making plans for us both——" she stammered.

Stella shrugged her shoulders.

"My good Karen, am I denying it? Kit played as underhand a trick on you as he did on me; worse, in a way, because he owed you no grudge, and I'm quite willing to admit that he did me. Now, he's got the grace to be rather ashamed of himself—or rather, he doesn't like being put in the wrong. So he's making the best of it and trying to atone, if you like such a melodramatic word, for having treated you badly. He hasn't said so, of course, but I've known Kit too long not to be able to read him like a book. Ever since he was a little boy, he has hated having to admit he was in the wrong. He has to be on top or he is miserable and, at the moment, because of you, he's feeling humiliated. If you think that is a foundation on which you and he can build a future, you are deliberately deceiving yourself!"

It was true! She had tried to blind herself to it, but really she had known all along.

"Well?" She heard Stella's voice coming from an immense distance. "What are you going to do?"

"What—can I do?" she answered slowly. "You and Christopher are both married."

"That can be undone—these days," Stella said casually,

lighting a cigarette. "Particularly in your case—a marriage that is no marriage at all!"

"Yes; I suppose so," Karen said very wearily.

"If," Stella said slowly, watching her through half-closed eyes, "if you really love him—you can make it quite easy. You've only to go away—and let him think you won't go through with it because he hasn't kept his part of the bargain."

"No!" Karen said, her voice harsh with pain. "I can't do that! He will think I am—what he thought I was at first!"

"What if he does?" Stella asked. "If he thinks you are nothing more than a girl who will do anything for money, he will feel that he owes you nothing more than money—and that is easily settled. He'll feel that he has the right to find real happiness for himself."

"Yes." Karen drew a deep breath. "I see."

"And you will do it?" For the first time Stella showed eagerness and Karen looked at her thoughtfully.

"Yes; I will do it," she said firmly. "For Christopher's sake. But—even though I go out of his life, I do not think that you will take my place."

"What nonsense!" Stella said loudly, as if, Karen thought, she had to convince herself that it was nonsense.

"Is it?" Karen was suddenly too weary to argue. "It doesn't matter. At least not now. But, Stella, what about Fred?"

Stella regained her poise with an odd abruptness.

"Fred?" she said carelessly. "Can you see him standing in the way of me being happy? I've only to convince him of that——"

She saw from Karen's face that she had gone too far, but there was no unsaying it.

"Well?" she said sulkily.

"Oh yes, I shall keep my word," Karen said quietly. "You have done so much harm already—or been the cause of it. This is at least one bit that I can undo."

"But how—and when?" Stella demanded.

"That is for me to decide," Karen said with a quiet dignity that was new to her. "And now, Stella, you must please find some way of persuading Fred to go home."

"Indeed!" Stella said scornfully. "And why?"

"Because for the little time that I am still mistress here I will not have you in the house." Karen spoke very quietly, but there was a scorn in her voice that pricked even Stella, for her eyes dropped and she said nothing and, after a moment, Karen went out of the room and left her alone.

Her plans were very simple. She would have preferred not to take anyone into her confidence, but she realised that since, sooner or later, legal steps would have to be taken, it must be possible for Christopher—or rather his solicitor—to get in touch with her. So, the simplest thing would be for her to go to Mr. Pilbright himself and explain the situation—at least, explain the lie that she had promised to tell and make it sound the truth.

Then, she would get a job somewhere—the harder the better, because then, perhaps, she would be too busy to think about Christopher. She smiled wryly, knowing what a forlorn hope that was, but at least being busy would be better than being idle.

Somehow Stella did persuade Fred that they must go home, and, to Karen's relief, she found herself alone in the big house. She explained to Mrs. Paynton that she was going to stay with friends for a time and that, as she would be moving about, all letters were to go to Mr. Pilbright's office.

Then she packed the simplest of her clothes and went up by train to London.

Mr. Pilbright looked slightly surprised when she was announced, but he welcomed her pleasantly and asked how Christopher had stood the journey to the nursing-home.

"Very well, thank you," Karen said gravely. "They rang me up to say that Mr. Braunton was quite pleased at his condition."

"And I suppose you will be going to see him soon?" Mr. Pilbright said for the sake of something to say. He was a man of considerable experience where difficult situations were concerned but he had to admit to himself that there was something wrong here, and because he had no idea what it might be, he found himself at a disadvantage.

"No," Karen said quietly. "That is what I have come to see you about. I am leaving my husband, Mr. Pilbright. You see, I really feel that he married me under false pretences. Oh, I know it was all in good faith on his part but the fact remains, things have turned out very differently from what we all expected, and—I am not prepared—not prepared——" She stopped, silent under his shrewd, penetrating eyes.

"Does Christopher know this yet?" he asked.

"No. I—you see, in spite of the fact that I know he will be relieved, I was afraid that it might be a shock—or that he might feel it was his duty to—to try to persuade me—and I will not be persuaded," she concluded firmly.

Mr. Pilbright pulled his long, thin nose, completely nonplussed. At last he had an inspiration.

"Well, whatever you are going to do in the future, you are going to spend to-night with Eleanor and me," he said with brisk firmness. Then he had a taxi telephoned for and helped Karen into it.

They sat in silence most of the way, each concerned with thoughts that could not be put into words. Then, with an impulsive gesture that startled Karen because it was so unlike him, he laid his thin old hand over hers and said with deep feeling:

"I cannot tell you how greatly distressed I am over what you have told me. Greatly distressed. After all, I am principally to blame for the fact that you and Christopher were married."

"Oh no," she assured him gently. "You brought us together. We made the decision for ourselves. There is no one else to blame." It was not true, but it was pointless to let this nice old man worry.

Miss Pilbright welcomed Karen in a matter-of-fact way as if it were not merely a matter of days since they had seen one another at Claverings. None the less, she was quick to sense the tension in the air and shot a swift, enquiring glance at her brother. He shrugged his shoulders and shook his head.

It was not until after dinner that Karen said quietly: "Have you told Miss Pilbright, Mr. Pilbright?"

To which he responded gruffly:

"No, my dear. I haven't. I'm still hoping that you are going to tell me that you have changed your mind."

"I'm sorry, but there is no chance of that," she said positively, and turned to his sister. "I have made up my mind that I am going to leave my husband, Miss Pilbright. I am not prepared to—to be his wife now that—he is going to get better."

"But you have done your best all along to help him get better," Miss Pilbright said helplessly. "Why did you do that if you felt this way about things?"

Karen said nothing. It was a discrepancy in her story that neither she nor Stella had realised was there, and she could find no satisfactory answer.

There was a long silence and then Miss Pilbright sighed. "Well, I must confess it is beyond me," she admitted. "Still, there it is. "Then—what are your plans?"

"I want to get a job."

"No need for that," Mr. Pilbright said shortly. "Christopher has made arrangements for you to draw as much as you like."

She shook her head vigorously.

"I can't take Christopher's money—now," she insisted.

"Nonsense! Now is just the time that you should," he told her. "And, after all, you've got every right to it. As you said, it was in good faith, but the fact remains that Christopher did marry you under false pretences. You have every justification in making him pay for that."

"Mr. Pilbright!" Karen exclaimed indignantly. "What a horrible thing to say! Surely, you don't think I would do a thing like that! I cannot take Christopher's money—now. I must get work."

"H'm." He took off his pince-nez and polished them furiously. "Well, you get it yourself, young woman. I've made enough mess of your affairs!"

"No, dear Mr. Pilbright!" she insisted earnestly. "It wasn't your fault things have turned out this way."

He was still not convinced, but what more could Karen say? For the time being, as if by common consent, they dropped the subject, but, a little later, when Karen had gone up to bed, he turned testily to his sister.

"Well, what do you make of it?"

Miss Pilbright shrugged her shoulders.

"It doesn't seem to make sense, does it?" she said mildly.

"*Seem* to make sense!" he said irritably. "It isn't sense! If ever a girl was head over heels in love, she is. And yet, the moment Christopher is out of the way, she calmly walks out on him—women!" he ended exasperatedly.

"Don't be absurd, Aubrey," she said placidly folding up her needlework. "You've only got to read between the lines and it is perfectly clear. Something has happened which has convinced Karen that Christopher would be better off—happier, without her. The only question is, what."

"Oh!" he said blankly. "Yes, I see. Well, what?"

"I don't know." Miss Pilbright spoke thoughtfully. "But I have an idea what it could be. The difficulty is proving it. Because you won't get any assistance from Karen."

"Of course, it might just be that she has had an attack of inferiority complex," he suggested.

"I detest that phrase," Miss Pilbright snorted. "It simply doesn't mean anything at all! Besides, after Christopher went, you heard her arrange with Miss Sarah that she would do something to polish up her social graces. Not that they need it, but she thought they did—and she was satisfied that they could be. Now she is convinced that there is nothing to be done about it and their marriage is on the rocks. Well, doesn't that tell you anything?" she demanded sharply.

"No; it doesn't. If she had seen Christopher again—or spoken to him. But she hasn't."

"Oh—Christopher! No, he has had nothing to do with this. You really can't see?" she fixed him with her little bright, bird's eyes. "Then really, Aubrey, I don't think you deserve to be told! Leave the rest to me!"

"I've little choice," he said crossly and sighed. "Eleanor, you—you like her, don't you?"

"If you must know, I've never been so fond of a young person in all my life," his sister said quietly. "She is a very dear child."

"Ah, then you'll do your best for her," he said with

satisfaction, and felt content that anything she might do would be in Karen's best interest.

If Stella had found Fred boring before, how much more so did he seem now that they were in their own home! It had always seemed queer to her that, while Fred should have a title, Kit should have all the money, but then Kit was the son of a younger son who had had to look after himself and had succeeded in doing so very well, whereas Fred had succeeded to an estate doubly impoverished by two lots of Death Duties in a comparatively short time. Not that it worried him. His tastes were simple and he preferred a quiet life in the country to one in Town.

Yet, oddly enough, when he told her that he had to spend a few days in Town, she felt no inclination to go with him. Or was it so odd? After all, the country without Fred was at least one better than Town with him.

But even so she was unable to settle to anything. A week or more of Kit's month at the nursing-home had passed, and soon things must come to a head. And Stella was uneasy. She had heard nothing at all from Karen—but then, she had not really expected to. All the same, she wished that she knew exactly what the girl had done. So, too, did Miss Sarah. She arrived on foot one morning and bluntly asked Stella where Karen was.

"My dear Aunt Sarah, I haven't the least idea. Do you mean to say that she hasn't had the good manners to tell you what she is doing?"

"I had a letter from her simply saying that she had changed her mind, and as she did not give me an address there was nothing that I could do about it," Miss Sarah explained. She shook her head. "It's so unlike Karen."

"But is it?" Stella asked thoughtfully. "I mean, after all, what do we know about her? She appeared out of the blue and, as far as one can discover, has always been some sort of a servant—nursing or something. That doesn't give us very much to go on."

"That isn't the sort of information I should think of allowing to sway my opinions," Miss Sarah said brusquely. "What I do know about her is that all the time she was at

157

Claverings she appears to have done all and more than could be expected of her for Christopher."

"It was rather to her advantage that she should," Stella suggested softly.

"And that the servants all adored her," Miss Sarah went on as if she had not heard the comment. "That is always a thing that tells." And she looked at Stella meaningly.

Stella shrugged her shoulders.

"That, of course, is meant to be a dig at me," she said calmly. "But—if you feel that Karen is such a mass of perfections, surely you believe that she must have some good reason of her own even though she has been rather discourteous to you."

"Oh, I'm not worrying about my feelings," the old lady assured her. "When you are as old as I am, you will know that it is rarely worth while taking offence. No; what I am worrying about is Karen. In some ways, although she has had to knock about in the world earning her living, she is a singularly unsophisticated girl. I hope no harm has come to her."

"I shouldn't think so for a minute," Stella said lightly. "My opinion of her is that she is very capable of looking after herself. Still, don't let that influence you. What do you propose doing?"

But Miss Sarah seemed to be lost in thought and for a moment she did not speak. When she did, it was not to answer Stella's question, but to ask one of her own.

"Stella, do you think that Karen has left Christopher? I mean, in the sense of wanting to break up their marriage?"

Stella drew a a deep breath. She must be careful.

"I think it is possible," she said judicially. "But I am no more in a position to give you a definite answer than you are."

"H'm. Is she writing to Christopher, do you know?" Miss Sarah asked.

"I don't know. I haven't seen him. But she did say——" Stella halted, realising that she was on the brink of saying a lot too much. "She said that Kit had asked her not to come and see him. Probably she realised what that meant."

"What did it mean?" Miss Sarah asked, fixing her relentlessly with her her small bright eyes.

Stella shrugged her shoulders.

"Why, that Kit wishes to goodness he had never done this mad thing and that she won't be able to get much more out of it, so she is cutting her losses and getting out now."

Miss Sarah's expression grew curious.

"You never liked her, did you, Stella?" she said thoughtfully. "Now, I wonder why?"

Stella waved impatiently.

"I've always been very fond of Kit," she said evenly. "It hasn't given me much pleasure to see him make a complete fool of himself."

"And of you—and Fred," Miss Sarah suggested softly, and had the satisfaction of seeing the flash of anger that Stella could not keep from showing. "Karen is his natural heir now, you know!"

"At present," Stella snapped and then, recovering her self-control, she laughed lightly, "Dear me, Aunt Sarah, are you still of the opinion that Kit married Karen in order to score off me?"

"Well, according to your own showing, it wasn't because he loved her," Miss Sarah pointed out. "So there must have been some other reason, mustn't there? Well, I must be getting back," Miss Sarah got up abruptly. "Is Fred to be away long?"

"He did not quite know how long," Stella said, accompanying her to the door.

The old lady had hardly gone before one of the maids brought in to Stella a letter from Fred. She slit it open indifferently, but the first few words arrested her attention. He began baldly and jerkily:

"To-day I met Ben Stringer. He told me that he had let you know about Kit's crash almost as soon as it had happened. Before you met me, in fact.

"I wish to God I were dead. I keep trying to think things over calmly, but I can't.

"I am going away, Stella. I would have sworn that nothing could ever kill my love for you, but this has and we can't go on now that it has happened. We had better make a clean break. I will give you the necessary evidence and I hope that, realising the irrevocability of my action, you will not ask me to continue a life that would be built on sham and fraud.

FRED"

She folded up the letter and put it back mechanically into its envelope. This really was most annoying! Of all the bad luck that Fred should just happen to meet Ben Stringer!

Suddenly her face cleared, and with an eager, impatient movement, she tore the letter out of the envelope again.

Fred's rather big, untidy writing straggled on to two pages. And each one was headed with the name of the hotel at which he was staying. She read each page through carefully and then laid them down side by side on a table. Then she picked up the second page. By chance it started with the announcement that he was going away, and without that other sheet it appeared to be an absolutely complete letter without the first page.

Stella's lips curved to a little smile as she carefully replaced the second sheet into the envelope. The first one she crumpled up and threw into the fire.

To Christopher it was the strangest month of his whole life. At first he knew that he was really afraid. He wanted so desperately to live now that he could hope to make life as full or even fuller than it had been before his accident.

He had told Karen that he would come back a different person, and that was perfectly true. Everything seemed so much more vivid now because he had so nearly lost all that made life worth living.

On the day that he was to return home, Cullen and Bannister were to come to the nursing-home for him with the car. For the time being Forster Braunton had advised him not to drive.

"Your nerves may not be quite as good as you think yet," he pointed out. "And we don't want any more crashes."

He was not to hunt, either, or do anything that might jar his spine. But that was only for the time being. In the future, he would gradually be able to do more and more, and in the meantime he did not feel that life would be empty. He had to wipe out the wrong that he had done Karen and that, he sometimes thought, would not be easy.

He had written her a brief note, which he had sent to Claverings, telling her when he would be arriving and asking her to wait for him there and not come to the home for him.

But as soon as he was settled in the car with Bannister beside him, he turned to the man.

"How is Mrs. Thirlby?" he asked.

Bannister hesitated.

"Well, man. Go on!" he said impatiently and then, as Bannister still did not reply, he caught him by the arm. "Nothing wrong, is there?"

"I hope not, sir. But—I thought you would know. Madam left Claverings a few days after you did, sir. And she has not come back!"

"Not come back!" Christopher exclaimed. "But—she had my letter. She knew that I was coming home. Damn it, I sent it to Pilbright with instructions to let her have it at once. He was keeping in touch with her while she was away!"

"As to that, I couldn't say, sir. But there is a letter in Madam's handwriting awaiting you at the house. It arrived this morning."

Christopher did not reply. There was probably some simple explanation. She had got held up, somehow. Perhaps an air passage or something had been cancelled. Or she might not be very fit and couldn't travel. For the first time since he had left home he began to doubt the wisdom of his decision that they should not correspond nor see one another, although at the time it had seemed the best thing to do. Now he realised that anything might have happened. Suddenly he realised the truth of Braunton's comment that his nerves might not be as good as he thought. Impatiently, he leaned forward and touched Cullen on the shoulder.

"For Heaven's sake step on it!" he ordered, and sank back in his seat to watch the flying landscape with eyes that saw nothing.

He had laid his plans so carefully. If Karen had been a different type of girl, he might not have given his orders as he had, but he had relied upon her doing as she was told. Now he was not so sure. Supposing she had somehow or other taken the law into her own hands.

In spite of the warnings he had received, he ran up the steps to the front door, which opened as he reached it. Mrs. Paynton was standing just inside ready to welcome him.

"Thanks, Mrs. Paynton," he said, trying to curb his impatience. "Yes, I'm glad to get back, but——"

Somebody emerged from the background and for the moment he thought that it was Karen. Then he saw that it was Stella.

"Kit, my dear!" she said softly. "I am afraid this is not much of a homecoming for you, but I wanted there to be someone here to welcome you!"

"Thanks, Stella," he said mechanically. "I want Karen's letter."

"Here it is." Stella took it up from the hall table and watched in silence while he read it. She saw the colour drain out of his face and put out a hand.

"Kit, what is it?" she said sharply. "Bad news?"

"Read it for yourself," he said thickly.

Stella took it, her eyes still on his face. Then she dropped them to the sheet of paper covered with Karen's childish handwriting:

"I'm very sorry, Christopher, but I can't go on. Things have turned out differently from what either of us thought and it just won't work. No marriage can that isn't built on love on both sides and ours isn't.

"I hope that when all this is tidied up you will be able to find real happiness—as I shall try to do.

KAREN"

"Well!" she said softly. "That seems explicit enough, doesn't it!"

"Not to me," he said grimly. "I don't understand it."

Stella laid down the letter and picked up her handbag.

"Kit, I'm afraid we've got to face up to it, you and I," she said gently. "A week or so ago, I received this from Fred. I think the two explain one another!"

CHAPTER ELEVEN

CHRISTOPHER read Fred's letter through twice before he handed it back to Stella and said:

"Well?" in a puzzled tone.

Stella took it from him and laid it beside Karen's. There was something almost symbolic in the way in which she paired them and it was not necessary for her to say, rather impatiently:

"Surely you can see!"

"You mean—Fred and Karen?" he said slowly. "But—that's absurd!"

"Is it?" she demanded. "Do you mean to say you haven't noticed how well they got on together? Karen is naturally rather a shy person, but would you say that she was shy with Fred?"

"No; she wasn't," he admitted. "But then, Fred is an easy sort of chap to get on with."

Stella checked her impatience with difficulty. How *could* he be so obstinately blind to the situation as she was presenting it?

"Kit, darling, I know it's all beastly, but—it won't do any good not to face up to things. It never does. Karen married you for the sake of the easy money that she thought she was going to get. Oh, don't think that I am blaming her! She has apparently had a hard life and it was the chance of a lifetime! And, more than likely, she had no idea what it really means to be in love — until she met Fred. Why don't you do what she suggests—cut your losses and start afresh."

"With you?" He spoke so tonelessly that she searched his face to see just what had prompted the question. But even then she was not sure.

"Why not?" she said recklessly. And then, as he did not reply she went on: "Kit, I played you a beastly trick. And my only excuse is that I did it in a mood of sheer panic. I'm not a heroine and I admit it. But then, I don't

164

think you are in much of a position to criticise me, are you? What you did was in cold blood and surely that makes it infinitely worse?"

"Perhaps," he admitted and Stella held her breath, her eyes narrowing. Had she said enough to convince him?

It seemed that she had for he rubbed the back of his hand over his eyes and said wearily:

"I don't know. This whole thing has got under my skin. Do you know what I mean when I say that I feel absolutely empty? I can't think properly and I can hardly feel.'

Stella bit her lip. This was worse than she had anticipated. She had the satisfaction, if you could call it that, of knowing that Kit believed the worst of Karen. But she had believed in all sincerity that his natural reaction would be relief that he could turn again to the girl he had loved before his accident—herself. And there was absolutely no sign of any such reaction. He was completely stunned.

All along she had realised that she would not have very long at her disposal. That she could only distort the truth in sufficiently plausible a way to convince him for the time being. But in that short time she was determined that Kit should so have committed himself to marrying her as soon as he was free of Karen that there could be no turning back.

She walked slowly over to him. Christopher had dropped into a chair and was sitting there hunched up in an attitude of complete dejection, staring sightlessly at nothing.

Stella went down on her knees beside him. She slipped her arms round his neck and laid her cheek against his. She felt him stiffen, but she paid no heed. In a low, passionate voice she said:

"Kit, this is our chance! Oh, I know, we've hurt each other horribly in the past, but it *is* the past. And it is only people who love as we do who are able to hurt like that. If you did not love me, what I did would not matter nearly so much to you. And I should not feel as if I had been stabbed to the heart because you married Karen. Kit, my darling, say that it isn't too late! Say that there is the rest of our lives for you and me!"

Her soft, pliant body was pressed against him and her

lips sought his. And surely, she told herself passionately, Kit's responded? They must have done! What man of flesh and blood could have resisted such an appeal?

Suddenly he stirred.

"Stella——" he began, and stopped because the door suddenly swung open and a faintly ironic voice commented:

"Dear me, I seem to have come at the wrong time!"

It was Miss Sarah, and she stood there surveying them with shrewd, bright eyes.

Christopher stood up and, disregarding Stella, walked over to his aunt.

"Aunt Sarah!" he said gently. "It was nice of you to come over to welcome me home!"

She gave his hand a little squeeze.

"It's good to see you on your feet again, boy!" she said with a depth of feeling that touched Christopher. "As a matter of fact, I might pretend to be cross because you flashed past my cottage in your car and didn't trouble to stop! But I won't tease you about that. I can understand you wanting to get straight home. You expected to find Karen here, of course? And you didn't?"

"No; she wasn't here," he said in a tone which suggested that only his affection for her kept him from asking her to mind her own business.

"But—Stella was!" she went on meaningly.

Stella jumped to her feet.

"Am I to be blamed if I took the trouble to be here to welcome Kit when nobody else did?" she asked shrilly.

"Am I blaming you?" Miss Sarah said blandly. "That was very wrong of me. It was a very gracious thing of you to do, particularly when you must have been so worried about Fred careering off to Scotland in that idiotic way."

"Scotland!" Stella said blankly. "What on earth made him go there?"

"Oh, there's an old schoolmaster of his who lives near Fife for whom Fred has always had a very great affection," Miss Sarah explained calmly. "Evidently he was seized with a sudden desire to see the man and just—went off."

Stella bit her lip. How like Fred to come back with a feeble story like this that simply aroused people's suspicions! And, of course, Kit would realise——

He did, immediately.

"Do you mean that Fred has been in Scotland with this man all the time? It doesn't make sense."

"And, anyhow, how do you know?" Stella demanded accusingly. "Don't believe her, Kit, it's all a lot of nonsense!"

"Is it?" Miss Sarah sat down placidly. "Well, if you don't believe it, I suggest you should ask Fred to prove it. It will be quite easy. He is down at my cottage now. Came last night, looking like his own ghost." She looked curiously from one face to the other.

"Well?" she asked.

"Stella thought—was afraid that Karen and Fred might have——" Christopher began, when his aunt interrupted him with a hoot of laughter.

"Gone away together? Never! Well, really, Stella, I think that is the most amazing fairy tale you've ever told in all your life. And you've told a few from time to time!"

"How dare you!" Stella said shrilly, her face white with fury. "It is a perfectly reasonable thing to think! Both of them going off suddenly like that, so close together."

Miss Sarah looked at her thoughtfully and then turned to Christopher.

"And did you believe it?" she asked gravely.

He hesitated, and then shrugged his shoulders.

"Has anything I have done given me the right to expect her to be faithful to me?" he asked bitterly.

"No; it hasn't," Miss Sarah said bluntly and yet in an oddly gentle way. "But then, some people are born lucky. And you are one of them, Christopher!"

"Do you mean that she——"

"I mean that the poor, silly little fool is head over heels in love with you," Miss Sarah said firmly. "And if you are too blind to see it, it's time an interfering old woman lent a hand!"

"It isn't true!" Stella said furiously. "She married Kit for his money——" She stopped abruptly, realising that

167

she had said too much in front of this shrewd old woman who was not to be confused, as Kit was, by the problem being too personal for clear vision.

"Did she, indeed?" Miss Sarah said caustically. "Then why did she do her very best to help Christopher get better?"

"Well, what did she do, if it comes to that?" Stella said recklessly. "She put up a show of being very much concerned, I admit, but what did it really amount to? Nothing more than pretending that he was drinking too much and trying to stop him! It was simply for effect, nothing else!"

"I see." Miss Sarah stole a look at Christopher, but he seemed to have nothing to say. None the less, something in the intensity with which he was staring at Stella prompted her to say caustically: "Then, if it was for his money, why did she leave him? Fred hasn't got anything like as much as Christopher, has he? So if money was her reason——"

"But Kit had settled a lot more on her—when he went into the nursing-home a month ago," Stella rushed on. "Don't you see, with that and—Fred's——" Her voice trailed to silence in the face of the sheer triumph in Miss Sarah's strong old face.

"I thought we had scotched the Fred myth," she commented. "But never mind, we'll leave that for the time being and concentrate on the money question. I gather that it would surprise you very much to know that not only has Karen not touched a penny of Christopher's money, but— she has taken a job!"

"What?" Christopher said sharply. "Aunt Sarah, are you sure of that?"

"Quite sure," she said placidly. "If you don't believe me, ask the Pilbrights. When she left here, she went straight to them and from there to this job. In the South of England, somewhere, I believe," she added pointedly. "Quite a long way away from Scotland."

"I don't believe it——" Stella began, but neither Miss Sarah nor Christopher heard her.

"She also left all the jewellery you gave her with Mr. Pilbright," Miss Sarah went on softly.

Christopher gave a short, hard laugh.

"So she couldn't stand having a single thing of mine to remind her!" he said bitterly.

"She kept her wedding ring."

"Did she?" Christopher said, almost under his breath. And then, urgently: "That means something, doesn't it, Aunt Sarah?"

"It does, my dear," she admitted. "But I am not going to commit myself to saying how much. You see, the child loved you—there is no doubt about that. But it is possible to kill love."

"I know," Christopher said, unaware that he glanced at Stella. He seemed to be lost in thought for a moment, then he said eagerly: "You did say that the Pilbrights have her address, didn't you?"

"I didn't say so. But they have. The only question is, will they give it to you?"

"Of course they will!" he said with a touch of his old arrogance. "They'll have to—and, anyhow, why shouldn't they?"

"Well, there are two reasons," Miss Sarah said carefully. "One is that they think you have treated Karen badly and they happen to be very fond of her. And besides that, Mr. Pilbright told me that he had promised not to tell you. Karen made him."

"Oh—I see," he said blankly. "Do you think—if I convinced them that—she would come to no harm from me, they would tell me?"

"That's for you to find out," she said gravely, and he nodded.

"Yes; I see. Very well, I will."

"Kit, you can't!" Stella protested. "Think of it, you, of all people, humbling yourself to a little nonentity like that! You can't do it! You'd never respect yourself again!"

"I shall never respect myself if I don't," he told her dispassionately. Then he laid his hand on Miss Sarah's shoulder. "Aunt Sarah, bless you for what you've done—and for your faith in Karen. But now—will you leave Stella and me alone for a little while? There are things that have got to be said."

Miss Sarah nodded, stood on tiptoe to kiss Christopher's cheek and whispered, "Good luck, my dear!" before she trotted out of the room without a glance at Stella.

And Stella? She stood lounging against the fireplace, and nobody who did not know her would have guessed the disappointment and fury that possessed her. She had lost, and she knew it.

Christopher came over very slowly to where she stood and, with his hands deep in his pockets, regarded her thoughtfully.

"Queer how one can know people for years and yet—never know them," he said meditatively. "There was a time when I would have sworn that you were—everything in the world that I wanted."

She swayed towards him.

"I'm still the same person, Kit," she whispered.

"Oh no," he said coolly. "You're not—and neither am I."

"It isn't true!" she said passionately. "We love one another—and you know it."

"No; I don't know it. And now I am beginning to wonder if it was ever true. Still, that doesn't matter now. Nothing about you and me together matters now."

"It does! It does!" She was almost weeping with frustration and fury. "I can't believe you can have forgotten."

"I haven't," he admitted. "I wish I could. One doesn't enjoy remembering that one was a somewhat callow fool!"

"Kit!" She stared at him open-mouthed, and he gazed back dispassionately.

"I should have liked to spare you this," he said slowly. "But I am afraid that it has to be said. All this time, you've been telling yourself that I went to extravagant lengths to revenge myself on you and that I love you just as extravagantly."

"So you did!" she insisted. "Look at the way you made Zelia dress Karen just like me. And the jewellery you made her wear! Oh, of course, that was for my benefit. You can't deny it, Kit!"

"No," he admitted. "I can't. But," he went on, ignoring her little cry of triumph, "you had hardly been in the house an hour before I realised what a fool I had been to worry about having lost you when I had lost something far more valuable than anything that you could ever give me."

He spoke deliberately, brutally, but Stella did not flinch. She even looked faintly amused.

"And what was that?" she asked lightly.

He did not answer immediately, and when he did it was not to give her a direct reply.

"Long ago, Fred and I realised that we both loved you. And, of course, we realised that one of us had to be lucky and the other accept defeat. I don't suppose you have any conception what the sort of friendship that Fred and I have for one another means. No; you couldn't. It's too deep a feeling for you to be able to appreciate. But at least you can understand this, that in spite of all the differences of character between us, we knew that we had something that we could not spare from our lives. So—we made a pact."

"About me?" she asked, leaning forward smilingly. It flattered her to realise just how disturbing the two men had found her.

"About you," he agreed. "We promised each other that, whoever married you, it should make no difference to our friendship. And that loyalty to the lucky one's wife should be unquestionable. There was something else. That we would play an absolutely straight game to each other in trying to win you." He laughed gratingly. "It all sounds rather young and idealistic now. But rather charming, don't you think?"

"Yes," she agreed mechanically. "Oh, yes."

"Well, can't you see what I mean?" He paused, waiting until she had shaken her head before he continued, ironically: "No? My dear Stella, aren't you a little dense? Don't you see that, although until then I had only thought of what you had done, when I came face to face with the two of you, I realised that it was what Fred had done that mattered far more. Fred, whom I had trusted all my life! I think if I had been able, I would have killed him and myself too!"

"Because he had taken me from you!" she said exultantly, as if that proved what she would have him believe.

"Oh, no," he said deliberately. "But because in marrying you like that, he had killed our friendship. There could never be the same love and trust between us."

Stella yawned delicately.

"You know, Kit," she commented judicially, "there are times when I really feel afraid that you are becoming dull and prosy! You really mustn't let it grow on you, my dear!"

"I won't," he promised. "Well, do you understand now?"

She shook her head.

"I'm afraid not, Kit. Perhaps I *am* dense, but you seem to me to have been giving vent to just a lot of sentimental twaddle—nothing more!"

"How inexcusable of me!" he spoke ironically, pausing to light a cigarette before he went on: "I must mend my ways and make myself clearer. When you first came here, you were more important than Fred. Then it was he whom I wanted to punish. And, finally, I realised that, incredible though it sounded, he had really known nothing about my accident. But the hellish thing was that, in spite of that, it was he who was going to be punished—and not by me."

She realised then what he was going to say, and he saw that she braced herself as if to withstand an actual, physical shock.

"Poor devil! He had married you—and no punishment I might have devised could equal that. You see," he went on reflectively, "when one has loved a person as I loved you and then that love is killed, it is possible to see them clearly perhaps for the first time. And I saw you that way. And I knew that all that mattered was—that I should do everything in my power to see that he never guessed what sort of a woman it was that he had married."

Stella stared at him in horrified silence, her fingers pressed against her scarlet mouth, and slowly, deliberately, weighing each word, he went on:

"I, on the other hand, had married a girl who didn't know what it was to cheat. Right from the beginning, she played straight. Oh, you can say that it was worth her while, if you like. That makes no difference. It was I who dictated the terms of our marriage and she kept to them loyally. She gave me so much that I began to want more, and because I knew that I had absolutely no right to expect it, I got angry, and my anger against myself recoiled on her. At the end, just before I went away, I thought that she understood and that she promised——" He broke off, scowling perplexedly.

Stella laughed hysterically.

"And all the time, she was only waiting until you had turned your back before she walked out on you!" she said venomously. "Oh, Kit, you fool. You've lost her! Take my word for that! For one reason or another, she'll never come back to you!"

"Perhaps not," he admitted, each word cutting like a knife. "But even if that is so, there is no place in my life for you, Stella!"

Then, it seemed, she really did understand that she had gambled and lost. The colour drained out of her face and she seemed to shrink as if, for the first time, she saw herself through his eyes.

"You'll never get her!" she panted fiercely. "I've seen to that! She'll never believe you!"

For a moment he hesitated as if he wondered whether it was worth while finding out just what she meant. Then, in a mood of utter revulsion, he felt that he could not stay with her for another second.

"I think," he said softly, "you had better hope that she does!"

Christopher drew up at the side of the road and consulted the map by the failing light. Impatiently he realised that he had contrived to lose his way and that he must retrace his course for about five miles to find the turning which he had missed. It meant that he would arrive at Nettlewick after dark, which would make the house where Karen was working even more difficult to find.

In spite of the advice he had received, he was driving himself, and if he had stopped to think he would have realised that he was tired. But other considerations were of more importance than that.

He had wasted time at the Pilbrights'. First of all, he had gone to Mr. Pilbright's office before he realised that it was Saturday and the office was closed. Then, when he had found him, Pilbright had been deliberately obstructive. In fact, he had refused point-blank to tell him where Karen was. And in the face of all arguments he had steadfastly kept silent.

"I promised her I would not tell you, and that is enough," he said firmly and from that stand neither blandishments nor threats would move him.

It was not until he was on the point of leaving, when Pilbright, before stumping out of the room, had told him that he did not care if Christopher did transfer the Claverings work to another solicitor, that Miss Pilbright came into the picture.

Christopher turned to her in desperation.

"Miss Pilbright, won't you help me?" he begged. "Don't you see that this is our one chance? God knows what devilment Stella has got up to, and if Karen *knows* that I am coming, as your brother suggests, she'll have time to prepare herself."

"And you think *your* one chance is to catch her unawares?" She spoke grimly, but Christopher saw that, though her eyes were watchful, there was something encouraging in them as well.

"Yes," he said shortly.

"That's honest at any rate! Now, tell me this, why do you want Karen?"

"Why?" he burst out. "Isn't it obvious? Because I love her! Because I want to share the rest of my life with her and—because I dare to believe that she loves me!"

"Yes," she said slowly. "It isn't going to be just as easy as that, Christopher, but—those are the only reasons that would justify me; my brother is under the impression that I also promised Karen I would not tell you where she is. As a matter of fact, I was not only very careful to give that impression, but equally careful not to commit myself in so many words. So my conscience is quite easy. Karen is acting as governess-companion to a Mrs. Avernden and her children. Her address is Beechgrove, Nettlewick.

And Nettlewick is on the Reading road fairly near to Thurley—— Well, really!" This latter remark came as she realised that she was speaking to the empty air. She watched Christopher climb back into the big car, and shook her head.

"I hope I've done right!" she thought anxiously. "I'll never forgive myself if I haven't! But what else could I do?"

And now, as Christopher turned the car and went back to search for the elusive turning, similar doubts were troubling him. Was he doing the right thing? Or ought he to have written to her, have been patient, have been content with slow, steady progress? Then he shook himself impatiently.

"No, by heavens!" he swore, unconscious that he spoke aloud. "She's mine and the sooner she knows I won't permit anything to come between us, the better!"

It was a drab, old-fashioned house, set back from the road and in considerable need of repair. Not, Christopher realised grimly, the sort of house whose owners were likely to pay a governess-companion more than the very least they could contrive to make her accept.

He knocked imperatively at the door, and after what seemed an eternity it was opened by a not too prepossessing maid.

"I want to see Mrs. Thirlby—at once," he said curtly, stepping into the hall before she could shut the door in his face, as he realised she was more than likely to do.

"I don't know. I'll ask the mistress——" she hedged, and scuttled down the passage-way.

"Hurry!" he shouted after her and possibly the sound of his voice as much as the maid's garbled story brought Mrs. Avernden into the hall in a very evident fury.

"How dare you come here shouting——" she began, but Christopher stopped her with a gesture.

"I've no time for the finer points of conventional behaviour," he told her brusquely. "I want my wife—Mrs. Thirlby—at once!"

"I do not allow my employees to have visitors—particularly male visitors."

"She is no longer your employee," Christopher insisted. "And, unless you tell me instantly where she is, I'll tear this damned house apart, brick by brick. Karen!"

He hurried over to the stairs, down which Karen was slowly walking. She stopped a little way from the bottom and he never forgot the picture that she made there in her plain dress, her soft grey eyes luminous in her pale face. Her lips parted.

"Oh—Christopher—you're well—you can walk," she whispered exultantly.

His heart leapt because her first thought was for him, and he held out his arms, regardless of the disapproving woman who stood behind him.

"My darling, I've come for you," he said softly, and instantly she shrank back.

"No, no, Christopher! You shouldn't have come! I—I quite understand everything and—I'll do just what you want me to! Only you must go——"

"Not without you." He spoke grimly because he was afraid. So sweet, so little and yet so strong and stubborn when she believed that she was doing the right thing!

"I can't come." She glanced at Mrs. Avernden, who raised her thin eyebrows.

"On the contrary, Mrs. Thirlby, you cannot stay! After such an exhibition, I insist that you go at once! Your clothes will be sent on after you—carriage forward, of course!"

"I think you had better come," Christopher said quietly, careful to keep any suggestion of triumph out of his voice, and, indeed, he was not sure that he felt triumphant. It was too early to know—yet.

Karen hesitated. Then she nodded.

"Very well," she said wearily. "I'll just go and get my coat and a few things."

Ten minutes later they were in the car. Silently, Christopher tucked a big, soft rug round her, acutely conscious of her sweet nearness and equally aware of her being withdrawn from him. Her white lids drooped and she would not meet his eyes. Only as he released the brake she asked, breathlessly:

"Where are we going?"

And with grim determination he replied:

"On our honeymoon!"

He drove in silence for over two hours and then, as if the route were quite familiar to him, he turned off the main road, and a few minutes later drew up in front of a dimly lit house.

He got out and came round to her side of the car.

"This is where we shall stay to-night," he told her in a voice that brooked no argument. She got out as he released her from the rug and shivered a little as she stepped out into the frost-hardened road.

It was not until afterwards that she learned he had brought her to a famous old inn that in a still more distant past had been a farmhouse and still retained some of its earlier characteristics. Its whitewashed walls still had polished copper farm utensils hung up on them, and the low oak beams suggested a house built for hard wear rather than for the entertainment of the stranger.

But Christopher was obviously no stranger. He was greeted with pleasure, though he had evidently not been expected.

"Why, Mr. Thirlby, we heard that you had had an accident!" A stout, cheerful woman came bustling forward to greet them, one curious eye on Karen.

"So I did. But I'm better," he said, shaking her by the hand. "Now, Mrs. Sweetapple, my wife and I are going to be stranded unless we can have a room here. What about it?"

"Why, of course!" she said heartily. "And dinner?"

"Dinner—later," he ordered. "I'd like a fire in our room."

"Why, Mr. Thirlby, when did you know me stingy on fires!" Mrs. Sweetapple said indignantly. "There's a log fire in every room in the house, weather like this! Come along, now, madam. You look real pinched!"

There was, as she had promised, a fire in the room to which they were shown and a generous one at that. Karen went instinctively towards it and held out her hands to the comforting blaze. Christopher, by the door, exchanged a few pleasantries with their hostess, and then Karen heard the door close and she knew that he was coming nearer to her.

"Now then!" he said quietly.

She turned instantly.

"Christopher, please don't—don't let's make a scene! I—you see, I know everything that you've got to say!"

He surveyed her quizzically.

"Do you, indeed?" he said drily. "All right, tell me what I was intending to say!"

"That you love Stella and—and you want your freedom." She spoke steadily, standing very erect, her hands behind her back like a little girl saying a well-learned lesson.

Christopher laughed and caught her in his arms.

"You precious little idiot!" he whispered tenderly. "Who told you that? No; stay still. You won't come to any harm! Now then, who told you that? Stella, by any chance?"

She did not reply and he went on:

"I suppose it never occurred to you that she might be making suggestions to me—about you?"

"About me?" She stopped struggling and her head went up. "But there was nothing to tell!"

"That would not stop Stella saying them, my sweet, believe me!"

He saw the bewilderment in her eyes, and if there were any last lingering drops of the poison that Stella had tried to instil into him, it went at that second.

"But what?" she demanded. "I don't understand."

"Oh—just that you and Fred were in love! And that it was wicked of me to keep you tied to me from pity!"

"But that isn't true," she said indignantly. "Fred is a dear—the sort of person you can't help loving because he is so nice. But in love—no! Stella knows that. She knows that I am in love with——"

"Yes?" very softly. "With whom?"

"With you," she said steadfastly and quickly added: "But you don't have to worry about that—or pretend."

"I'm not pretending. I love you," he insisted.

Karen shook her head.

"Christopher, dear, there are some things that one can't pretend about," she said gently. "And this is one of them. I do understand. I think I did almost from the beginning. And I understand, too, that you were—ashamed of what you had done and wanted to give me a chance to —to learn things so that I could go about and not disgrace you."

"What?" he shouted. "Where the devil did you get that idea?"

She looked at him wide-eyed.

"Why—just before you left in the ambulance. You told me to go about and meet people. You said that it would give us the best chance——"

"But, good Lord, that wasn't what I meant!" he insisted, his hands gripping her shoulders. "Child, you can't have thought I was such a cad. What I meant was—don't you see, I knew by then I loved you and—I was desperately afraid! You were my wife—but that was cold comfort! I wanted your love, and it seemed to me that the only thing I could do was to make you accept all the freedom I possibly could so that you would not feel you were trapped. Then, when I came back—perhaps you would have let me teach you to love me," he finished humbly.

He saw the quiver of her sensitive lips and knew that he had touched her deeply. But again she shook her head.

"Christopher, dear, you mustn't worry so about me," she said gently. "I know you feel you've got to put things right, but this isn't the way. More than anything in the world, I want you to be happy. I know you're angry with Stella, but in your heart of hearts, you love her. I've always known that!"

"She happens to be Fred's wife," he commented, never taking his eyes from her expressive face.

"I know. But—that is not my business. All I can do is— step aside. For the rest——"

"If I did not love you, I could beat you!" he said in exasperation. "Listen, I do not love Stella!"

"Oh yes," she said fatalistically. "She was quite right. You proved it."

"And how did I prove it?" he asked with as much patience as he could muster.

"You loved her so much that, seeing her in danger, you could make that tremendous effort to get up," she said simply.

He gave a wordless little exclamation.

"And you think that proves I love Stella?"

"I think so."

Christopher laughed softly, triumphantly.

"Now I have got you! Listen, beloved, did Stella happen to tell you whether I said anything when she screamed?"

"No," she admitted listlessly.

"Just one word," he said very quietly. "Your name. You see, I thought it *was* you!"

CHAPTER TWELVE

"CHRISTOPHER!"

She held him away, her hands pressed against his shoulders so that she might look into his face, and in her grey eyes he saw incredulity and dawning joy struggling for mastery.

"It's true," he said, his voice unsteady with the intensity of his feeling. "Remember—you were both wearing red dresses, you are both dark. I was lying half asleep thinking about you, and all of a sudden I heard a scream. I didn't stop to think. You were in my mind, and it never occurred to me that it could be anyone but you in danger of a horrible death, with no one there but me to do something about it. I *had* to get up. But not for Stella. For you."

For a long minute she searched his face, and he waited, hardly daring to breathe, praying that she would believe him.

Then, quite suddenly, she capitulated. Her head went down on his shoulder, her hands locked behind his head, and he knew that he had won. Yet, because of all that had happened, he was almost afraid to claim her. Very gently, he turned her face up to his and, for the first time, their lips met.

And, after that, there were no doubts left. Something that had been starved and denied all her life awakened to full growth in Karen, and in the sweet, quivering passion of her soft lips and her utter surrender to the mastery of his arms Christopher experienced a triumph such as he had never known before. A triumph—and a humility. He had married this girl simply to make use of her and out of that marriage he had received nothing but good. All the happiness in the world lay in her hands, and humbly he knew that she would never deny him the wealth of it. It was her nature to give as, perhaps, it was his to take. But none the less, he could give too. Because of her, he was a new man, and the love that he could give her was as fresh and

181

unsullied as if Stella had never existed. He swore silently that it always should be and that never again through him should she suffer. Her happiness was something that he would cherish all the more because, in his selfishness, he had been so indifferent to it.

He looked down at her tranquil, happy face and her smile made his heart turn over with gratitude and delight. She was his, utterly, entirely his! His arms tightened.

"Tell me what you were thinking about," he demanded.

Her smile deepened, taking on a mischievous quality.

"You will be cross," she warned.

"Shall I? I doubt it. At the moment I don't feel as if I could ever be cross again!"

"Very well, then. I was thinking that—I am dreadfully hungry!"

He chuckled appreciatively.

"Karenhappuch, you are a little wretch! I thought you were going to tell me that you thought I was the most handsome man in the world, and all you have to say is that you are hungry!"

"Well, aren't you?" she demanded.

He considered.

"Now that I come to think of it, I am," he admitted. "Come on. Let's do something about it!"

Like a boy, he was prepared to dash down immediately, pulling her by the hand, but she protested laughingly.

"I must do my hair. You've ruffled it dreadfully!"

"Well, what's it matter?" he wanted to know. "It looks charming. And, besides, even if you tidy it, people will still know."

"How?" she wanted to know.

He drew her to him again.

"Your eyes, beloved," he said unsteadily. "And if you look at me like that, I shall have to kiss you again!"

"Oh, Christopher!" He felt the answering flame in her and caught her to him again.

When, finally, they did get downstairs, all the other diners had finished and they had the warm old room to themselves. What they ate they had no idea, but, in spite of Karen's protests, Christopher ordered champagne and insisted on her drinking a little on this special occasion.

"You must," he insisted. "We've got to drink the health of the bride and bridegroom!"

So, obediently, she lifted the glass that he filled and softly echoed his words:

"To the happiness of Mr. and Mrs. Christopher Thirlby!"

They stayed at Hundred Acre Inn for the best part of a month—a month, Christopher insisted, that was worth all the rest of his life up to that date.

"In fact," he told her, "I don't think I was ever really alive before!"

Bannister drove down one day with more clothes for both of them, but in spite of his very sympathetic delight in their happiness he did not stay.

"He's a good chap. One of the best. But, at the moment, I don't want anybody, however sympathetic. I want it to be—just us!

"Just us," she echoed contentedly.

Karen was a changed person these days. To Christopher it was a constant delight to watch her quick, instantaneous friendliness wih the people that chance brought to the inn. She must, actually, always have been like that, he realised; but now, secure in his love, for the first time in her life she was unafraid, and because of it she blossomed like a rose.

There were times when he wished that they need not go back to Claverings. From what Bannister had told him, he knew that Fred and Stella were together again, and he shrank from taking Karen back to the surroundings in which she had been so unhappy. In his heart of hearts, he knew that he was still afraid lest he should lose his new found happiness, and he was reluctant even to discuss the necessity for meeting his cousin and his wife just as if nothing had happened. It was, he knew, the only way in which the situation could be made bearable, since they all lived so close together, but it was a lot to ask of Karen.

So it was somewhat to his relief when she herself brought the question up.

"Christopher," she said one day after a long silence. "Does Fred know, do you think?"

"Why Stella married him, you mean?" He hesitated. He himself had realised from Fred's letter to Stella that he did know now, and that it had been a terrible shock to him. But Karen was ignorant of that letter or that Fred had ever left Stella, and it might be wiser never to let her hear of it.

While he was still hesitating she went on earnestly:

"Because what I was thinking is that, if he does know, then he would much rather not know that we do as well. It would—save him feeling humiliated, I think."

He lifted the hand that he was holding to his lips.

"Do you know, Mrs. Thirlby," he said gravely, "that not only are you a very sweet young person, but also a very wise one. Yes; you are quite right. If he knows, then it would leave him with at least some sort of dignity if he believes that we don't. Poor old Fred," he ended with a sigh.

"He loves her a tremendous lot. Perhaps that is enough," Karen suggested, but there was a degree of doubt in her tone that made him say:

"Yes, go on. Finish what you were thinking about."

"Just that, as I spoke, I knew that it wasn't enough. It has to be both people, loving with all their hearts, to be enough."

"Like us?" he suggested.

"Like us," she agreed.

They came back to Claverings on a crisply frosty morning that yet seemed to hold a promise of the spring to come. And this time they went in together.

Miss Sarah was there to welcome them, and so were the Pilbrights. Both the older women hugged Karen as if she were their own daughter and even Mr. Pilbright so far unbent as to kiss her warmly on the cheek. With Christopher he shook hands and asked quizzically:

"Well, have you forgiven me?"

Christopher grinned.

"I suppose so. All the same, thank Heaven women have a different standard of morals from men!"

"Quite," Mr. Pilbright agreed. "Utterly lacking in logic, of course, and mentally incapable of appreciating the legal and even moral obligations of a promise. But still—thank Heaven, as you say!"

"Fred and Stella were to have been here," Miss Sarah commented a little anxiously. "But the road is worse over that side than the one you used. Probably it is taking them longer than they estimated."

As if in reply, they heard another car drive up, and a minute later Fred and Stella came in.

Unconsciously, Christopher braced himself and felt Karen's small warm hand slip into his, but whether to seek comfort or to give it he did not stop to think. His own hand closed firmly round it and he felt an answering pressure,

And, after all, they need not have worried themselves how best to cope with what might be an embarrassing situation, for Stella took it in her stride and set the keynote of the future then and there.

She came sweeping towards them, beautiful in her furs and the *chic* little scarlet hat that perched on her dark hair.

"Darlings, how very naughty you have been!" she said blithely. "Running away like that. But we shall have to forgive you because you both look so idyllically happy. Don't they, Fred darling?'

She slipped her arm through Fred's and gave it a little hug.

"Yes; they certainly do," he agreed.

Stella rubbed her cheek against his coat sleeve.

"Almost as happy as we are, my sweet," she went on. And then, dropping his arm, she went to Karen and kissed her on both cheeks.

"You and I are very lucky women," she confided gaily. "It isn't every woman who marries the man she loves!"

Christopher heard the quick catch of Karen's breath, and involuntarily he turned to see what Fred's reactions were to this palpable lie.

But to his amazement there was absolutely nothing in Fred's bearing to suggest either disbelief or distress. If anything, his usual amiability seemed to be deepened to genuine pleasure at this evidence of friendship between the two girls. And, to Christopher's puzzled eyes, there even seemed to be a new dignity about Fred.

He began to doubt the truth of his own convictions. Had he misjudged Stella? Had she realised, after all, that she loved Fred? Or was she acting a part in order to save her own face?

She was clever enough to do that, he firmly believed, but—how about Fred? Had she beguiled him into believing that she loved him? Or—did he know that it was all pretence, yet accepted the situation because he had neither the courage nor the desire to live without her?

But Christopher thrust that thought out of his mind. He could not bear to think of the man he had loved all his life being humiliated and degraded to that degree.

No; Stella must have convinced him that she cared and, for Fred's sake, they must all hope that he was never undeceived—if it was a deception.

But, after all, why should it be? Fred was a kindly, easy-going soul and deeply in love with his wife. Surely it was possible that late, but none the less sincerely, Stella had learned to appreciate his value—perhaps, even, Christopher's own brutal outspokenness had had something to do with it.

He did not know and he never would, for it must remain Fred's secret, and he himself must keep a constant watch on his tongue. Loyalty to Fred demanded that. But he knew that the old frankness and freedom between the two of them was gone for ever. Stella and what she had done stood between them.

For Christopher himself there was Karen, and so long as he had her everything else was of secondary importance.

And then, suddenly, he grew afraid. After all, what right had he to such good fortune? He wasn't nearly such a decent chap as Fred. He was arrogant, selfish, inclined to put his own desires before everything else. Why should she love him?

He looked towards her, seeking reassurance, but she was talking to Miss Sarah and he could not catch her eye. He went over to her and stood behind her, waiting until Miss Sarah drifted away to talk to Fred.

Karen put up her hand and drew his down over her shoulder.

"Yes?" she murmured softly.

"Just I wanted to make sure that you love me," he whispered.

He felt the little tremor of emotion that ran through her. Then she turned her head slightly and the softness of her lips brushed against his hand.

THE OMNIBUS
Has Arrived!

A GREAT NEW IDEA
From HARLEQUIN

OMNIBUS

The 3-in-1 HARLEQUIN — only $1.95 per volume

Here is a great new exciting idea from Harlequin. THREE GREAT ROMANCES — complete and unabridged — BY THE SAME AUTHOR — in one deluxe paperback volume — for the unbelievably low price of only $1.95 per volume.

We have chosen some of the finest works of world-famous authors and reprinted them in the 3-in-1 Omnibus. Almost 600 pages of pure entertainment for just $1.95. A TRULY "JUMBO" READ!

The following pages list some of the exciting novels in this series.

Climb aboard the Harlequin Omnibus now! The coupon below is provided for your convenience in ordering.

Catherine Airlie

Omnibus

This author's fine books have become famous throughout North America, and are greatly anticipated by readers of romance all over the world. The three stories chosen for this volume highlight her unusual talent of combining the elements of compassion and suspense in one exceptional novel.

. . . . CONTAINING:

DOCTOR OVERBOARD . . . on board a luxury liner, cruising between the Canary Islands, Trinidad and Barbados, a young Scot, Mairi Finlay, is facing a traumatic experience, torn between her growing affection for the young ship's surgeon, and her duty to her employer who has set her an impossible task . . . (#979).

NOBODY'S CHILD . . . from London England, we are taken to a medieval castle, the Schloss Lamberg, situated on the outskirts of the City of Vienna, to brush shoulders with the aristocracy of the music world. Amidst all of this beauty, a young girl, Christine Dainton, is submerged in the romance of a lifetime with one of the most admired men in the world . . . (#1258).

A WIND SIGHING . . . Jean Lorimer's life has always been happy here, on the small Hebridean Island of Kinnail, owned by the Lorimer family for centuries. Now, Jean and her mother are grief stricken on the death of her father. They will surely lose their home too, for Kinnail was always inherited by the eldest male in the family, whose arrival they expect any day now (#1328).

$1.95 per volume

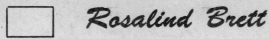

Rosalind Brett

Omnibus

A writer with an excitingly different appeal that transports the reader on a journey of enchantment to far-off places where warm, human people live in true to life circumstances, Miss Brett's refreshing touch to the age-old story of love, continues to fascinate her ever-increasing number of faithful readers.

. . . . CONTAINING:

THE GIRL AT WHITE DRIFT . . . Jerry Lake had travelled from England to Canada to live with her unknown guardian, Dave Farren. On arrival, Mr. Farren drove Jerry to his home, White Drift Farm, explaining that a few months' farm life would strengthen and build a fine body. To her utter horror, Jerry realized that this man thought she was a boy! . . . (#1101).

WINDS OF ENCHANTMENT . . . in Kanos, Africa, in surroundings of intense heat, oppressive jungle, insects and fever, Pat Brading faces the heartbreak of losing her father. The acute depression and shock she suffers in the following months gradually subside, and slowly she becomes aware that she is now married to a man who revolts her and whom she must somehow, escape . . . (#1176).

BRITTLE BONDAGE . . . when Venetia wrote the letter which had brought Blake Garrard immediately to her side in a time of need, she had felt great sorrow and bewilderment. Now, some time and a great deal of pain later, it was the contents of another letter which must drive her away from him. Only now, Blake was her husband . . . (#1319).

$1.95 per volume

Sara Seale
Omnibus

Her natural talent for creating the very finest in romantic fiction has been acknowledged and enjoyed by a great many readers since early in Miss Seale's career. Here, we have chosen three perfect examples of her best loved and most cherished stories.

. . . . CONTAINING:

QUEEN OF HEARTS . . . when Selina presented herself to her new employer at Barn Close, the exclusive country hotel in Coney Combe, Devonshire, Max Savant had one thought: to send this "child" on her way. Now, it was impossible for him to imagine himself or his hotel being without her. But he must, for he has just become engaged to Val Proctor . . . (#1324).

PENNY PLAIN . . . at Plovers Farm, near the village of Chode, in England, Miss Emma Clay is employed as assistant and companion to the rather spoilt young lady, Mariam Mills. Their relationship proves to be rather stormy, not the least cause of which is the country vet in his country tweeds, the uncompromising Max Grainger . . . (#1197).

GREEN GIRL . . . Harriet listened to the incredible suggestion that she marry this total stranger and thus solve her dilemma, and the trouble which he himself was in. Whilst she knew full well that her own plight was quite hopeless, instinct warned her that Duff Lonnegan's trouble was far more serious than even he knew . . . (#1045).

$1.95 per volume